Doubt at Daytona

Other books by Ken Stuckey
Slowdown at Sears Point

Doubt at Daytona

Ken Stuckey

Baker Books

A Division of Baker Book House Co
Grand Rapids, Michigan 49516

Published by Baker Books
a division of Baker Book House Company
P.O. Box 6287, Grand Rapids, MI 49516-6287

Printed in the United States of America

Library of Congress Cataloging-in-Publication Data

Stuckey, Ken
    Doubt at Daytona / Ken Stuckey.
        p.   cm.
    Sequel to: Slowdown at Sears Point
    Summary: Two teenage boys who share an interest in stock car racing and God return to the NASCAR circuit at the Daytona 500 race.
     ISBN 0-8010-4300-X
    [1. Daytona 500 (Automobile race) Fiction. 2. Stock car racing Fiction. 3. Christian life Fiction.] I. Title.
    PZ7.S93757Do 1999   99–41341
    [Fic]—dc21

For current information about all releases from Baker Book House, visit our web site:

http://www.bakerbooks.com

Dedication

THANKS, GING. Without you so many things would not have been possible. I appreciate you. You are a precious gift from the Lord.

In his heart a man plans his course, but the Lord determines his steps.

Proverbs 16:9

"If you aren't driving on the egde you are using up too much track."

Buddy Baker, retired stock car racer

ORLY MANN SAT in quiet contemplation with his gloved hands resting comfortably in his lap. He was used to waiting, and he liked nothing better than sitting inside his race car while he did it. It was his world and his alone. It was also one of the few places in the real world where he was comfortable. The form-fitting seat that was built to the specifications of his body—and his only—added to his comfort. Orly was a man of few pretenses, and the interior of his race car was a place where hype ended and reality took over. He was a race car driver in a business that

7

forced him to have a public image that satisfied sponsors and fans and was built very much on outward appearances. His driver's suit was a walking billboard for all of the sponsors who paid tribute to be seen on him and his race car. But when he climbed through the window of his car in the classic stockcar manner—left leg first, then the right, then a quick push on the roof with both hands—it was into the world of brutal reality. No amount of hype would get him out of trouble at 200 miles per hour surrounded by forty of his closest friends.

Orly was, for the moment at least, content. Contentment did not necessarily mean relaxed, however. To the casual observer he might look placid and maybe even a little bored sitting deep in the interior of the orange and yellow race car. In truth he was not relaxed at all but was as tightly wound as one of the thick coil springs that made up the suspension of his 3,600-pound machine. It was Saturday, the first day of qualifying for America's race—the Daytona 500. It was NASCAR's most prestigious and lucrative race of the year, and Orly wasn't quite sure what to expect. But then this was racing and the unexpected was common. He was parked in a row of brilliantly painted and numbered "stock cars" that were anything but stock. They were unique, full-out thoroughbred race cars, designed to look like the ones Mom and Pop drove to the grocery store, minus the numbers, decals, and paint jobs, of course. Underneath that thin outer skin rested a tubular chassis and engine that were truly state of the art and designed to make the thing go as fast as the wind with a blast of bellowing thunder through open exhaust pipes.

Orly was waiting for his turn to race the clock for two hair-raising, gut-wrenching laps to determine his starting position for the qualifying races on Thursday. Unlike the NFL, which has its Super Bowl at the end of the season, NASCAR begins the race for the Winston Cup Championship series with a weeklong festival of speed and excitement in Daytona Beach, Florida. The week culminates on Sunday with the running of the granddaddy of them all—the Daytona 500. The 500 is the richest race of the year for the competitors, with an enormous amount of prize money to be spread through the field. On Sunday, over two hundred thousand people position themselves around the two-and-a-half-mile track in stacks of grandstands that seem to reach the sky. Winston Cup racing outdraws football and baseball combined, and this is the first race of the year. The fans and drivers are eager to get the season under way. The satellite feeds and media crews take the TV pictures and radio broadcasts to untold millions around the world, and the winner of the battle becomes an instant celebrity, featured on talk shows and media blitzes. That, of course, is secondary to the fact that he will also fill his pockets with a little over a million bucks.

Right now, all that didn't matter much to Orly as he casually wiped a drop of sweat out of the corner of his eye with one gloved finger and contemplated the overcast sky. It was gray and muggy, and the air seemed heavy and moist. He wondered if they had missed the setup on his car. The orange and yellow #37 Chevrolet seemed to be fast, and the Orly Mann Racing Team had used the off-season, short as it was, to do some serious testing and modifying. But the question was . . . was it fast enough? Racing, at least

Winston Cup racing, was not so much about speed as it was about competition. It wasn't so much a question of how fast you could go as it was, Could you go faster than the other guys? The thing that drew the fans year after year was the neck-and-neck, fender-on-fender, swapping-the-lead, tight-as-all-get-out, side-by-side competition.

The track was unique. When Bill France built the thing in the late fifties folks were agog. It was huge. A lap around the Daytona International Speedway was two and one-half miles from start to finish. The track was built in the shape of a tri-oval with thirty-one-degree banking in the turns. Thirty-one degrees doesn't sound like much, but it is so steep that an ordinary person has a difficult time walking up from the bottom of the track to the outer wall. There is a four-story difference between the apron, or bottom, of the track, and the concrete outer wall at the top. The front straight has a little dogleg in it, which is what makes it a tri-oval, and it is banked fifteen degrees. The start-finish line sits right in the middle of the dogleg with the flagman's box hanging high out over the track. It is 1,900 feet, or more than one-third of a mile, from the flag station at the start-finish line back to the middle of the corners. The back straight is a long, flat 3,800 feet and gives the drivers plenty of time to run flat out at over 200 miles an hour. It also gives them plenty of time to contemplate the steep banking as they approach turns three and four. Because of this banking drivers seldom, if ever, use the brakes. The only way to get a decent qualifying time is to keep your foot flat on the floor for the whole lap. It is not a place for the fainthearted. In fact, if speed scares you then you'd better load up the hauler and head home.

The place was fast, and whoever qualified fastest would probably have an average speed of somewhere over 193 miles per hour. The last guy to qualify would be no more than a second or two slower. Just a couple of ticks off the clock. It was not unusual for the first ten qualifiers to all be within several hundredths of each other, which meant they would be racing so close together you could throw a blanket over them. There was a reason for that—mostly because NASCAR liked it that way. It was called "restrictor-plate" racing. Some drivers liked it, and some had nightmares about it.

Orly had yet to run anywhere near the fastest speeds posted in practice, because his team was concentrating on the race setup, but they would see. In racing language they were "chasin'" the track a little right now in terms of their qualifying setup and speed. The car was okay but in racing terms it wasn't "good." Too late now, though. They would have to make do with what they had, or as Bear put it, "throw something against the wall to see if it would stick." Yes, indeed, they certainly *would* see in a few minutes.

Orly looked out the left side of the car as Bear walked up and put his head inside. Bear started to say something but changed his mind. He slapped the roof of the car with both hands and turned away, pulling the ever-present red shop rag from his back pocket to mop his sweating forehead. Bear didn't like muggy weather much.

Bear was Orly's partner, crew chief, and best friend. He was also about as opposite in personality to Orly as possible. Orly always seemed calm and in control and moved with an economy of motion as if every gesture and step were carefully planned. Bear, whose given name was

Henry Erickson, always seemed to be in a constant state of ebb and flow. Some part of him never stayed put for very long, and he could seldom sit still for more than a few minutes. He was a graduate of a large southern university with a degree in engineering and understood the sport of stock car racing better than most anyone. He also had several degrees from the School of Hard Knocks and not only understood the racing business but also what made it tick.

Bear neither looked nor acted like his nickname. In fact, the name "Bear" had been affectionately given to him a number of years ago by some crew members, led by Bud Prescott, who were victims of his idiosyncrasies. When Orly would come thundering into the pits during the heat of battle for a splash of fuel and fresh tires, Bear would challenge the crew with the admonition, "We got to bear down now, boys; we got to bear down." It wasn't long before the crew changed Henry's name to Bear, and Bear liked it. He always signed his autographs, "Bear down," with a little picture of a bear's face underneath.

And bearing down was something Bear's crew did better than most. They were expected to give it everything they had and make the pit stop as quick and efficient as possible, something they usually did in sixteen to eighteen carefully choreographed seconds. That's why some editor in the press had tagged them the Thunderfoot Ballet Company a few years ago. It was a name they secretly relished because it gave them a sense of notoriety and set them apart from the other teams. It also made them work all the harder to be quicker and better than anyone else.

Bear was a worrier, which seemed to be a necessary prerequisite for crew chiefs in any type of racing. Today he was a little more worried than usual. He walked away from the car and sat on the pit wall, contemplating the nearly full grandstands across the racetrack. Looking to his left, he saw a media crew approaching the line of cars waiting for their turn to qualify.

NASCAR had become a media darling in the past few years, and fan clubs numbering in the thousands made drivers and crews as popular as movie stars. TV crews had become part of the NASCAR landscape, and this crew was making its way with its cables and camera through the line of cars. The blond commentator, seeing Orly's window net down, paused and said into the microphone, "Sitting patiently in his car is two-time Winston Cup champion Orly Mann. He hasn't had much luck here at Daytona the past few years. He had a decent season last year, winning one race and finishing thirteenth in the overall standings. He has never won the Daytona 500, but maybe this year is his year. He hasn't shown much speed in practice so far, but let's see if we can get a word with him."

He turned toward Orly and asked, "Well, Orly, how's the car today? Do you think you have a realistic shot at the pole?" Then he thrust the microphone in Orly's face.

"Well, Bob, I don't know," Orly said with a weak smile. "Anything is possible, but the truth is, I don't think we've found the right combination for qualifying. We have put most of our efforts into trying to get our race setup right, but we'll see what happens." Orly forced a broader grin and looked into the camera.

The commentator pulled the microphone out of the car and spoke into it again: "Say, Orly, I wonder if you would tell the folks at home what it would mean to you to win the Daytona 500? You've had a pretty good career but haven't won the big one yet." He stuck the mike back in Orly's face.

"Well, Bob, I don't rightly know what to say. Sure I'd like to win the Daytona 500, but show me any of these guys out here who wouldn't. To win here, you got to have just the right combination of speed, handling, plus, as you know, a little help from your friends. A win here is pretty special. Besides that, it pays a lot of money and gives a team a great jump on the year. Come Sunday, we'll see how it all plays out. I expect the 125 Qualifier on Thursday will give us some indication of what we got."

"There you have it folks. Thanks, Orly," the commentator said into his mike while looking over the cameraman's shoulder at the next car in line.

Bear waited until the crew was finished, then stuck his head back in the window and spoke quietly to Orly.

"What does he know. Just because we haven't done very well here don't mean we don't know about racin'. Those guys give me a pain. I guess winning the champeenship twice don't mean nothin' either." Orly merely grunted in reply.

The truth is that both Bear and Orly had a love-hate relationship with Daytona. Racewise they had done well here through the years but never well enough to win. Three years ago Orly was leading on the next to the last lap when he cut a tire down, handing the win to the very surprised second place driver. Orly had been so far out in front, the guy knew he never had a chance at catching him. By the time the crew got the tire changed Orly was relegated back to twenty-third, which was a long way from winning.

Daytona also was the site of the worst crash and the most pain that Orly had ever endured. He was rubbed—bumped hard—by another car coming off of turn four and slid into the wall. The impact wasn't anything spectacular, but it bounced Orly back across the track out of control. He wound up sitting dead skunk, stopped in the middle of the exit of the turn, facing the oncoming traffic. A group of cars racing hard with each other came off the corner three wide, and the middle car had no choice. He dynamited the brakes but still t-boned Orly's car at over 140 miles per hour.

Orly could still picture the crash in his mind. He remembered watching the grille get bigger as the car approached him, almost in slow motion. He could even make out the paint chips on the lower part of the front air dam, and then his world erupted in a brutal explosion of screeching sparks and smoke. Mercifully, he blacked out with the impact. They had to cut him out of the twisted wreckage with the hydraulic Jaws of Life, and he awoke to find his leg broken in two places. After three surgeries and a pile of screws and steel rods, the doctors were able to put him back together, but he still walked with a slight limp when he was tired.

After the crash NASCAR implemented some rule changes that affected the structure of the roll cages and side bars, but even those changes wouldn't have helped Orly much. The leg still hurt on occasion, especially on muggy days, but Orly never complained. Racing was his life, and it was a given that every driver took a hard shot now and then if he stayed in the sport long enough. It seemed odd to a lot of folks that Orly would continue to race after getting hurt so badly, but they didn't understand. It was much like a football player going through knee reconstruction and then coming back to play again. There was always that chance of winning the Super Bowl. Of course, football players usually didn't run the risk of getting killed. Orly loved racing and he didn't want to do anything different. At least not for now.

"You think we made the right decision, Orly?" Bear asked.

"Yeah, I think so, Bear. You know we don't have a chance of making the front row. But once we get through qualifying and everybody starts running their race setup, we'll be right in the thick of it. Stop worrying, Bear."

"You know I can't do that, Orly. It's part of my nature," said Bear, grinning.

"You and Paolo make a great pair, I tell ya'. With the two of you there's enough worrying going on to roof the racetrack. You guys remind me of that old dog Bud used to have that had nine pups and couldn't keep track of them all," Orly said.

"Now Orly, you know I don't fret much. I don't know why you'd say such a thing," said Bear with a frown.

Orly looked up at Bear's furrowed brow and said, "Yeah, right."

Bear ignored Orly's comment and glanced to the back of the race car where Paolo Pellegrini was busily wiping away nonexistent dust from the gleaming paint with a soft rag. He was a big kid with curly black hair and an olive complexion and was dressed in an orange and yellow Orly Mann Racing Team uniform. As always, his shirttail was hanging out. His brow was furrowed as he smoothed a microscopic bubble out of the wax with his fingernail.

"Yeah, he worries a lot, but he's a good kid and a hard worker. Him and Doug do a good job for us," said Bear. Then he changed the subject. "Now, Orly, I want you to be extra careful with those shocks we got on. I don't like them soft things. If you get this thing sideways," Bear slapped the roof of the car, "it could get pretty hairy."

The slap on the roof panel made the air flaps jump. They were small, aerodynamic panels that looked like oversized mailslots in a door. They were built into the roof of the car to keep the car stuck on the ground if it got turned around. When the cars went forward, all the aerodynamics worked like they were supposed to. But if the cars got sideways and then spun backward, they had a tendency to act like a huge airplane wing and try to fly. Orly could testify that the flaps worked pretty good.

The difference between a qualifying run against the clock and a race setup was like the difference between a 100-yard dash and a marathon. Qualifying at Daytona didn't mean quite as much as it did at other racetracks. Usually the cars did one or two laps around the track against the clock, and the fastest car started on the pole. Here at Daytona, the only positions that were guaranteed were the two spots on the front row of the grid. After posting qualifying times the field was divided in half, and two qualifying races were run the Thursday before Sunday's big race. Sunday's race was 500 miles, or 200 laps around the two-and-a-half-mile track. Thursday's races were 125-

mile sprints and could be brutal affairs as everybody was jockeying for a starting spot in the big race. How a driver finished the 125 determined where he started on Sunday. The big problem at Daytona was that there were always more cars trying to qualify than there were qualifying positions. If a car had engine or handling problems or got caught in a wreck, a team might as well load up the transporter and head home—they were done for the weekend.

There were other variables to qualifying, but the best way to make the race was to qualify the best you could and then go like thunder in the 125.

Unless, of course, you were a past champion. A past champion was guaranteed a provisional starting spot at any race. The only problem with a provisional starting spot was that it put you dead last on the starting grid, or close to it, and that wasn't a good place to start any race, let alone Daytona. Orly was indeed a past champion, twice in fact, but he sure didn't want to start dead last. Coming through the pack and trying to work your way to the front took incredible skill and courage at this racetrack, plus a whole bucketful of good breaks.

Paolo was thinking about restrictor-plate racing as he polished the car. A few years ago NASCAR officials and the tire company representatives and others began worrying about the escalating speeds at Daytona and NASCAR's other superspeedway in Talladega, Alabama. As the crews worked harder in development and the engines became more sophisticated and powerful, the speed of the cars kept creeping upward. Catastrophe was just around the corner. NASCAR's concern wasn't so much for the drivers as it was fear for the spectators and other innocent bystanders. Higher speeds meant greater stress on machinery, particularly the tires. If a tire came apart or a car broke mechanically at the wrong time, there was the possibility of a car going airborne in the wrong part of the racetrack and hurting somebody. The solution to slowing the cars was both simple and diabolical.

Internal combustion engines generate power with the proper combination of the three elements—air, fire, and fuel. The carburetor blends air and fuel. It mixes the proper amount of gasoline with the proper amount of air and sends it to the combustion chambers in the cylinders. More air and fuel mixed with the proper amount of spark equals more power. Less air and fuel means less power.

NASCAR solved the problem by making every car use a mandatory restrictor plate between the carburetor and the manifold. It restricted the amount of air and fuel the engine could suck in, which effectively reduced a 700-horsepower Winston Cup car engine to something around 450. Bear called them "little wienie boy" motors. They might be restricted, but they still generated enough horsepower to push the cars over 200 miles per hour. *Man, that is fast*, thought Paolo. The first time he saw a pack of cars thundering down the back chute and heading into turn three it nearly took his breath away. They were really moving and they were running incredibly close together. He had seen it many times on TV, but there was no comparison. When you could hear the sound for real and see how close the cars were to each other . . . it was awesome.

Restrictor plates did their job exceedingly well, but they also radically changed the dynamics of superspeedway racing. The plates had a tendency to equalize the competition, which made all the cars run together and kept them bunched up. One driver said it was similar to racing in an overcrowded subway car during rush hour—no room to breathe. It was extremely difficult to put distance between yourself and the competition. The potential for disaster was multiplied, and nearly every "restrictor" race had one, if not several, multicar wrecks. Orly's crash at Daytona had been a direct result of this type of racing. He was running in the middle of a large pack of cars when somebody just flat made a mistake.

Paolo glanced over and saw Bear with his head in the window of the car talking to Orly. Bear stepped back and looked down the pit lane. He could see the officials getting ready, so it wouldn't be long till qualifying started.

Meanwhile, across the country in south-central California, Juan-Jesus Lopez Mendoza was cold and very tired. The cold wind off the Chocolate Mountains blew across the desert with a nonchalance that sliced right through his coat like it didn't exist and made his thin thirteen-year-old body shiver. He put his hands in the pockets of his worn jeans, hunched his shoulders, and backed against the wall of the building. The bricks were still a little warm from the hot afternoon sun, but the wind would cool them in a hurry. As hot as the desert could be during the daytime, it could be equally as cold at night. Last night Juan-Jesus had found shelter in a concrete culvert but he was still miserably cold.

He was also very hungry. He hadn't eaten anything except for two cold tortillas in two days. He had to eat soon. Any sudden movement made him dizzy, and he didn't have much reserve in his small body. At least he wasn't thirsty. Not like yesterday. He mentally thanked God he still had a plastic quart bottle of water in the threadbare backpack hanging off his thin shoulders. He had filled it in the rest room of the truck stop a while ago. He didn't want to go through that again. He hadn't realized how precious water was until he didn't have it. Now he was two days from home on foot and very scared and uncertain as to what his next move should be. He stood silently and prayed.

Juan-Jesus had kissed his mama good-bye while she was sleeping yesterday in the predawn darkness. She had looked so tired, snoring softly on the old mattress in the little shack. They lived on the southern side of the bustling city of Mexicali, Mexico, next to the canal. It was only when Juan-Jesus's mother was sleeping that her face was overcome with the burden of care she carried. Mostly she tried to smile and be an encouragement to her children, but Juan-Jesus knew better. Their shack was in a poor section of town, almost in the country. There was no electricity and no running water except that in the canal. Juan-Jesus was no longer even conscious of the odor that drifted up from the green scummy water that flowed lazily by in the ditch only a few feet from the door of the shack.

He had left his mama a note on the table and then kissed his two little sisters. He would miss Maria and Angelica very much. Maria was ten and Angelica was eight. He was the big brother and they adored him. Angelica had looked so pale in the early morning darkness. She was breathing heavily as she slept, but even in the pale moonlight Juan-Jesus could see the dark circles under her eyes. After Papa died, Mama had gone to work at the mercado, and Juan-Jesus spent much of his time taking care of his family. They needed him, and now they needed him more than ever. Things had not been so good lately.

Juan-Jesus had a plan that he hoped would make things a lot better. Well, it was sort of a plan. The first thing he had to do was cross the border into the *Estados Unidos*. He had never been across the border before, but many of his classmates had done it many times. They said it was simple if you didn't get caught. Then they told him it wasn't the Border Patrol he had to watch out for so much as the "coyotes" who preyed on the "illegals" who made the run across the border. If the Border Patrol caught him, they would just put him on a bus and send him back to Mexicali, especially since he was just a kid. If the coyotes caught him, they would steal everything he had and maybe beat him up or even worse. He had first thought about leaving home just after everyone went to bed and crossing the border at night, but the truth was he was just too scared. He decided to try at dawn when everyone might be a little sleepy. He'd managed to save five American dollars for his trip, but after thinking about it for a while, he had carefully laid three of the crumpled one-dollar bills on the table next to his note. Sadness had hung over him like a cloud as he trudged up the dirt road beside the canal to the highway. He had turned and looked over his shoulder at the shack where Mama and the girls were sleeping, but he hadn't been able to make out much in the dark. The tears in his eyes blurred his vision, but he gulped, took a few deep breaths, and kept going. He must do this; it was their only hope.

"Why, God, did you have to take Papa," Juan-Jesus asked to the darkness as he wiped the tears from his face.

Getting across the border had been a lot easier than he expected. He hopped a slow-moving freight train in the early morning darkness and sat on a flatcar with a bunch of other folks. People called the train the "poor people's bus line," and it wasn't unusual to have several hundred people hanging off the freight cars as they traveled through the city of Mexicali. The government tried to stop them, but some said it would be easier to stop the hot wind that blew in the summertime.

The city was just starting to wake up, but full dawn hadn't come quite yet. When the tracks made the bend next to the border, Juan-Jesus jumped off with a group of people all carrying bundles of some sort. They scattered in different directions, but Juan-Jesus walked along the tall fence with the *No Entrada* signs that marked the border. He could see the houses of Calexico through the holes in the fence, and in truth they didn't look much different than the houses in Mexicali. He spotted a hole in the wire just big enough for his small body, took off his backpack, turned sideways, and just like that was in the United States. A quick sprint across the road, then a little jog, and *bueno,* he was on a backstreet in Calexico, California.

Yes, crossing the border had been easy. It was the next part that got Juan-Jesus into trouble. He could have walked to the main highway leading out of Calexico and maybe hitched a ride, but now he was an illegal and worried about being picked up by the Border Patrol and sent back across the border. He had a tattered map in his backpack, and if he just headed north he'd hit Interstate 8. Interstate 8 would take him to Interstate 10, which stretched across the *Estados Unidos*. He needed to go east, and it didn't look too far to the interstate. His friends told him about a truck stop and marked it on the map for him. They told him truckers sometimes gave folks rides, and he hoped to find a trucker heading east and hitch a lift. So without thinking about it too much, he headed out of Calexico, walking across the open alfalfa fields.

It was easy going as Juan-Jesus crossed the fields, ducking under fences, and the early morning sunshine felt good as he walked through the fragrant grasses. A few miles later the terrain changed, and the green of the fields turned to the parched brown of the desert. It was amazing what water could do to fertile soil, and it was also amazing how dead everything looked without it. Making the trek to the interstate wasn't nearly as easy as it had looked on the map, and before long Juan-Jesus was far away from civilization and was very tired and very hungry. The terrain got rocky and uneven, and as the day progressed the desert turned from warm to hot, even at this time of year. February could be miserable. The wind came out of the north all day long, constantly blowing in his face. He couldn't help himself—every so often he would stop and look back to see his beloved Mexico. After a while it made him too sad, so he took a deep breath and forced himself to stop doing it. Sometime during the day he ate his two tortillas. Then, before he was ready, it began to get dark. He knew he was heading in the right direction because he could see the military jets flying in and out of the Marine base in El Centro. He would get to I-8 soon if he could just keep going.

As quickly as the sun began to set, the desert got cold. Really cold. Juan-Jesus was shivering uncontrollably. It was almost too dark to see when he stumbled upon a concrete culvert under a dry roadbed. The culvert was about three feet high with a layer of crusted dirt on the bottom, but at least it was dry and would protect him from the wind. He crawled in and huddled in the blackness. He tried to close his eyes but couldn't sleep. This was a good place for snakes and scorpions, and besides, he was very hungry and thirsty. He had started from home with a half-full, quart-size water bottle, but it wasn't nearly enough. Though he had tried to ration the water, it was gone by noon and his mouth and throat were dry. Tears rolled down his cheeks as he curled up with his arms wrapped around his body. The desert was full of strange sounds and rustlings. Once, when he thought he felt something crawling over him, he lay very still with his heart pounding in his chest.

It seemed that he was the only human being left on the face of the earth. A couple of times he felt the ball of fear in his stomach start to grow and shoot up the back of his throat. He was on the verge of panic, but he knew that the safest place for him would be right here . . . for now. He closed his eyes, clenched his hands tightly together, and prayed.

"Please, Lord Jesus, give me strength. I am so hungry and so very much afraid, Lord Jesus. Pastor Rojas said that you hear everyone who comes to you with a humble heart. Please, Lord Jesus, take care of my mama and sisters and give me courage, Lord Jesus. You know what I must do, and I can't do it without you. Please help me."

Mama had told him that prayer was the only thing that kept her going when Papa died. Pastor Rojas had told him that Jesus himself spent a lot of time praying, and that one time he prayed so hard it looked like he was sweating blood. That was just before Jesus went to the cross. Juan-Jesus continued to pray. The praying seemed to keep the fear away, but he was still very scared in the dark.

He dozed a little now and then, and each time he awoke he hoped to see the sun peeking over the mountains. After what seemed like an endless night, he finally did see the sun begin to come up over the mountains. He wasted no time crawling out of the culvert and forcing his aching, thirsty, and ravenously hungry body to move. The second day was kind of a blur, and he just kept putting one foot in front of the other. Just about the time he decided to give up hope, he saw in the distance the black ribbon of the interstate with its fast-flowing line of cars and trucks.

Two long hours later he was standing with his back against the brick wall of the truck stop restaurant. He had used the rest room to clean up and to fill his water bottle. The water tasted so good, and the warm water coming out of the tap soothed his windblown cheeks and hands. Now he was more hungry than he had ever been in his whole life. He still had the two dollars in his pocket, but it was all he had. He knew he might need it down the road, but he was on the verge of spending it anyway. He must eat ... and soon.

He crouched down on his haunches while he wrestled with what to do and watched a big burly trucker come out of the restaurant with a white bag in his hand. While Juan-Jesus watched, the man walked over to the bank of pay phones on the wall. He put the bag on the ground, reached for his wallet, and pulled out his calling card.

Juan-Jesus's mouth filled with saliva, and he licked his lips as his stomach growled yet again. He was so hungry. He eyed the white bag. Stealing the food would be wrong, but the aroma coming from the bag made his mouth water. It might be wrong, but it would be easy. He was only a few feet away. He could casually walk by, grab the bag, and make a run for it. The man had a large stomach that hung over his big belt buckle and he wouldn't miss the meal too much. He didn't look like he could run very fast either in those tall boots. No, Juan-Jesus couldn't do that. It was stealing, and the Bible said stealing was wrong. What was it Pastor Rojas said? "If we can trust God to give us salvation through his Son, Jesus, then we can trust him to meet our daily needs." God gave him a culvert to sleep in last nightn didn't he? Pastor Rojas taught many lessons about trusting God in the little board church in Colonia Televisora. Didn't the Lord's Prayer begin, "Give us this day our daily bread"? Remembering his prayers from the night before, Juan-Jesus bowed his head and prayed silently, "Father, I am hungry. Please give me something to eat. I haven't had any bread at all this day."

The trucker finished his phone call, hung up the phone, and started to walk away, leaving the bag on the concrete beneath the phones. Juan-Jesus's heart leaped in his chest and his stomach growled louder as he stared at the bag. But he made a quick decision and spoke before he could change his mind.

"Señor," he said and then pointed to the bag. The man stopped and turned around with a puzzled look on his face. He saw the bag, picked it up, and looked at Juan-Jesus.

He scowled and said, "Here, kid, you eat it. You are about the puniest looking piece of work I ever saw. You need this more'n me. Besides, my stomach don't feel so good and I'm not feeling very hungry right now." He patted his ample girth, then flipped the bag to Juan-Jesus and walked away.

Juan-Jesus didn't understand what the man said, but he deftly caught the bag with a *"Gracias,"* then bowed his head and said a quick prayer of thanks. He tore into the bag and found a large burger with the works along with onion rings and fries on the side, plus a large chocolate shake. He resisted the impulse to shove the food down his throat with both hands, instead eating slowly, chewing every mouthful. He'd been hungry before and knew that shoving food down quickly could make him sick. After the third bite he sat down on the curb and finished every crumb, licking his fingers in the process. While he was noisily sucking up the last bit of the shake, he glanced across the parking lot and saw the beautifully painted orange and yellow fifth-wheel trailer that was hooked to an equally beautiful orange Chevrolet pickup. Written on the side of the trailer in large letters was ORLY MANN RACING, DAYTONA BEACH, FLORIDA, CHARLOTTE, NORTH CAROLINA.

The word *Florida* jumped out at Juan-Jesus. The other words in English made no sense to him, but Florida was what he was looking for. Slowly he got to his feet and patted the bulge in his worn backpack.

didn't know about that, but he did know he was having the best time of his life. He and Doug met last year at Sears Point and had become great friends. Both of them had just graduated from high school then. Paolo had put in a semester at San Francisco State College in the fall, but his heart really wasn't in it. It wasn't that he didn't want to go to school, it was just that he wanted to do so many other things first. Mostly he wanted to be involved in the racing business. His time with Orly's team just whet his appetite, and now he wanted more hands-on experience.

One day, out of the blue, a phone call had come from Orly asking if he wanted to take a break from school and work a few months for his Winston Cup team. He would earn pretty good money and gain incredible experience. Paolo was so overwhelmed he could hardly carry on a conversation with Orly. Paolo saw it as an incredible gift from the Lord, and it was the most exciting thing that had ever happened to him in his whole life. He loved racing and had been a devoted fan since he was a little kid. He was intelligent, understood the nature of the sport, and was gifted with great mechanical aptitude. He was considering pursuing a degree in mechanical or design engineering, but not right away. Orly explained that Paolo would be working mostly as a gofer and traveling with the team. A gofer was lowest on the totem pole and spent most of his time "going for" stuff. He would also be called on to do anything around the shop to help the other guys out.

Doug called next, and he was as excited as Paolo. They would be working and traveling together. Doug asked Paolo if he wanted to share a little apartment above Doug's parents' garage in Charlotte, North Carolina. With Orly's shop fairly close-by, it would be great.

Although Paolo's parents were sad he was leaving, they were thrilled with him at this opportunity to work with Orly. They didn't really understand the "racin' biz," as Bear called it, but they were excited because he was excited.

The only one not so happy about Paolo's move to Charlotte was Alicia. When he told her he was leaving she got big tears in her beautiful, almond-shaped eyes and had to excuse herself for a few minutes. When she came back she was somewhat composed and tried bravely to be excited with him. Paolo and Alicia had been friends almost their entire lives. They had grown up in the same neighborhood and attended the same church. They didn't always see eye to eye and sometimes she drove him nuts, but he realized he'd taken her for granted. The night before he said good-bye she cried again, and Paolo found himself a lot sadder than he expected in leaving her. It would be weird not having her around.

He and Doug did quite well together, but Paolo was glad Mrs. Prescott invited them to supper fairly often. Doug's cooking skills were almost nonexistent, and Paolo was what Mrs. Prescott called "in process." They ate a lot of macaroni and cheese with hot dogs, and there was always plenty of cereal and ice cream. "Basic staples," they called them.

Paolo's time at the shop was great, and he could hardly wait to get to work in the morning. It was wonderful to finally be doing something he'd always wanted to do. Bear was the greatest teacher and even in the midst of the most difficult circumstances took time to tell Paolo what he was doing to the race car and why. Some of the other guys weren't so patient and gave him a hard time.

The crew never picked on Doug because his dad, Bud Prescott, was a senior member of the team. Bud was a man who knew what was what almost as well as Bear, and the respect the team afforded Bud spilled over to Doug. Paolo was amazed at the way Bud could take a piece of straight sheet metal and work it through the presses time after time so it was magically transformed into a perfectly formed fender panel. Then, with a few taps here and there, it fit just right. Bud's hands were like magic. Bud loved Doug very much, and as a result, he treated Paolo with good-natured camaraderie. Bud genuinely liked Paolo and did his best to teach him also.

Doug, on the other hand, didn't spend much time in the shop. Most often he was in the office with the other staff going through the computer printouts and handling the personnel and public relations stuff. Sometimes he worked as Orly's secretary, taking care of much of Orly's personal business. It took a lot of effort to keep the racing team going. Orly spent as much time at the shop as he could, but it seemed like he was always flying here or there to make a sponsor appearance or do some other business related to the team.

Doug and Paolo rode to the shop together but seldom spent time together during the day. Paolo worked hard and did what he was told. He hadn't yet earned respect from the other team members, but Bear told him that if he hung in there and did his job, it would come.

Paolo and Doug had been roommates for a month, but it seemed as if Paolo barely had gotten his stuff settled in before he was loading the brightly painted hauler with the rest of the crew and heading for Daytona Beach. The hauler was fresh from the paint shop, and when Jimmy drove it into the shop compound it brought instant attention. The hauler was a traveling billboard that announced to the whole world in brilliant colors that this was the Orly Mann Racing Team. It was designed to make a statement as it traveled the United States ten months of the year with the other Winston Cup teams. It was huge, and everything that wasn't painted was chrome. The cavernous trailer carried the primary race car, a backup, and enough parts to build a third. Spare engines, transmissions, rear-end gears, shocks, and suspension components all had their special places. It not only carried the race cars but everything needed to service them and the crew as well.

When Paolo watched Jimmy pull the thing into the compound, he could feel his heart begin pounding. As he walked around to examine the transporter, he nearly fainted and couldn't suppress a grin when he saw his name along with all the other crew members newly lettered in a small box below the cab.

This was Paolo's first race with the crew. He was nervous and very much afraid he might do something wrong. The first day they got to Daytona he was helping the guys unload the race car from the transporter when he turned around to see a TV cameraman a foot away from him, pointing a huge camera at him. It so unnerved him that he immediately blushed and looked away. Several of Orly's crew laughed at him as the red color crept up his face to the tip of his ears. In the process he dropped the armload of shop towels and other assorted odds and ends he was carrying and was immediately hung with the nickname Fumbles. From then on everyone except Doug, Bear, and Bud called him Fumbles. He had no choice but to take it good-naturedly, even though he didn't like it much. They could call him whatever they wanted. He was a paid member of a genuine full-fledged Winston Cup racing team owned and operated by none other than Orly Mann and his famous crew chief, Bear. If anyone didn't believe it, they could look on the side of the hauler—there was his name. Besides that, he had his own uniforms with *Paolo* over his left pocket. They could call him whatever they wanted.

Paolo finished tucking in his shirt, raised his chin, and looked at the crowd with a little defiance in his eyes. Man, all these people here just to watch qualifying. He did a slow turn and looked all around the racetrack. From the pit lane he could see almost all of the high-banked corners. Behind the pits was the infield, and behind that was Lake Lloyd and then the back straight. Paolo was beginning to understand just how big the Daytona facility was. *This place is enormous, and I bet it is going to be wild here on Sunday with a sold-out crowd,* he thought.

There was a stir of motion down the pit lane, and the silence of the afternoon was suddenly shattered by the guttural cough of a highly stressed qualifying motor coming to life. It grumbled to itself in a low murmur as the driver let it idle, then suddenly it roared with a crackling that reverberated off the grandstands. Qualifying had begun, and both Bear and Orly raised their heads and looked over the tops of the gaudily painted race cars to see the pit marshal wave the first car onto the track.

Juan-Jesus watched the club-cab pickup with the enclosed fifth-wheel trailer circle the parking lot and then come to rest in a slot next to the line of long-haul tractor trailers. Tyrone Wallace eased his body out of the truck, stretched his arms, and yawned.

"Coffee time with some supper," he muttered to himself. He locked the pickup and walked toward the restaurant with long strides. He was a big man with long arms and a bushy mustache that gave him a fierce, heavy-eyebrowed look. He glanced at Juan-Jesus standing on the curb, then quickly looked away with a sneer.

"Beggars—got no use for 'em. Thick as fleas on an old dog in this part of the country. Why don't their parents teach them kids to make a living at least?" he complained aloud to no one in particular.

Juan-Jesus looked again at the truck and trailer. Sure enough, it said "Florida" on the side. He followed the big man into the restaurant and waited patiently in the foyer, his eyes focused on the rest room door. The man finally came out and found a seat in the bustling dining room. Juan-Jesus waited for the right moment, then walked up to the edge of the booth where the man was sitting by himself looking at the menu. Juan-Jesus had rehearsed this moment over and over in his mind. His English was very limited, but he had memorized what he must say. He would courteously ask the man if he might have a ride to Florida on a mission of utmost urgency. He would be willing to work and could pay the man two dollars, which was all he had. Surely the man would be sympathetic. When the man said yes he would say, "Thank you very much," and they would be on their way. But it didn't work that way.

Juan-Jesus stood at the end of the table and the big man looked up and scowled at him from beneath the black, bushy eyebrows that were anything but friendly.

"Whatta you want, kid? You better not be asking me for money 'cause if you are, I'm going to get up and thump ya good," said the man in a deep voice.

The look on Tyrone's face and the fierce tone of his voice unnerved Juan-Jesus, and his memorized English vanished into thin air like fog in a windstorm. He managed to stammer out *"Senor,"* but it was all he could get out of his constricted throat as he wrung his hands in front of his worn pants.

Suddenly behind him a gentle voice spoke in Spanish. "What do you want, Chico? This hombre does not look so friendly. I wouldn't advise that you ask him for money," he heard her say.

Juan-Jesus turned around to see a Latino waitress with a coffeepot in her hand. She was plump and energetic, and while she spoke she deftly poured a cup of coffee and set it in front of Tyrone.

"I need to ask the man if he will give me a ride to Florida. I can work for him and I will give him two dollars. I know it is not much but it is all I have. It is very important that I get to Florida." The words flowed from Juan-Jesus in a soft rush.

The waitress looked at Juan-Jesus and raised her eyebrows in a universal Mexican Mom gesture. Then she spoke to the man in English.

"This kid wants a ride to Florida and says he can give you two dollars for the trip." Then she laughed and asked Tyrone what he wanted for dinner.

Tyrone paid no attention to the Spanish conversation between the waitress and the boy. It was none of his concern, and the only thing he was interested in was eating.

"Yeah, right," said Tyrone. Then he went on, "I think I'll have the chicken fried steak with the country gravy and an extra side of fries and a piece of cherry pie with ice cream on it."

The waitress said, "You got it," wrote the order in her book, and took the menu. She looked over her shoulder at Juan-Jesus and said sharply in Spanish, "You come with me."

Juan-Jesus dutifully followed her, not really understanding what was happening. The waitress turned in the order and then pulled Juan-Jesus by the collar of his thin jacket to a corner and spoke quietly but forcibly while she looked straight into his eyes.

"What is the matter with you, boy? You cannot go up to complete strangers and ask them for a ride across the United States. It is too dangerous. If that man had agreed to take you, I would have immediately called the police for your own protection. I don't know where you have come from or where you are going, but you better be careful. You are in the real world now, and it can be a dangerous place. If you are going to survive, you must protect yourself. Now get out of here before I call *La Migra* on you."

Then she reached into the pocket of her apron, counted out five dollars from her tips, and shoved it into the pocket of Juan-Jesus's coat.

"When you get the chance you contact your mama. I'm sure she is worried about you. Now get out of here." With that she was gone to pick up her orders.

At first Juan-Jesus was shocked by the waitress's stern words. He could give no response and just stood there blinking his eyes at her retreating back and fingering the money she had stuck in his pocket. Then she turned the corner into the kitchen and was gone. He stood there for just a minute more, then turned and walked out of the restaurant. The cold desert wind was blowing even stronger now that full darkness had fallen.

She is right, he thought. *It is a dangerous thing to do, asking a complete stranger for a ride.* There had to be another way. He studied the orange pickup and fifth-wheel trailer. What a gift the waitress had given him—first a warning and then the money. "Thank you, Lord," Juan-Jesus prayed silently.

When he thought no one was looking, Juan-Jesus ran across the parking lot to the shiny rig. He walked around the trailer and noticed it had a very large back door that looked like it might be a ramp of some sort. Then he noticed that on the right side it had a much smaller door that was probably used for access to the front of the trailer. Juan-Jesus studied the door for a minute, then quickly took off his backpack and pulled a worn leather tool kit from the inside pocket. The kit was about four-by-six inches in size and was made of thick leather with a snap to hold it together. He looked carefully at the inset lock on the door as he unsnapped the tool kit. "I am sorry, Papa, that I have to do this thing. You taught me that a locksmith must be an honest man or he is a disgrace to his trade, but

I think this is the only way. I will not steal anything. I am simply going to see about hitching a ride to Florida. Surely God would not be upset with me for that."

Pablo Mendoza had been considered one of the best locksmiths in the Mexicali Valley, and with his slow and meticulous style he taught Juan-Jesus the basics of his trade. The little tool kit had belonged to Juan-Jesus's papa, and it contained a set of picks and master keys for many lock manufacturers. It also contained a set of files and some brass key blanks. Juan-Jesus pulled what he needed from the kit, stood up quickly, and with a deft motion of his nimble fingers unlocked the door.

When the door opened a light went on inside the trailer, and he quickly saw that it contained a very shiny orange and yellow car with a large number 37 on the door. The car was anchored with a set of cables that held it snugly in place. It filled up most of the trailer, but there was still room to move around. Near the side door was a blue ice chest, and in the part of the trailer that hung over the pickup bed was an overhang with what looked like several tarps. It would make a nice bed, Juan-Jesus decided. Yes, this would work, but now he would have to work fast. The big man would finish his supper soon.

Juan-Jesus quickly walked back to the restaurant and went into the little store that was next to it. He bought two quart bottles of water and looked around for other supplies. Everything seemed so expensive. Maybe he could do better at the restaurant. He walked around the building to the back where the kitchen would be. Sure enough, there it was; and a Mexican man was standing nearby smoking a cigarette and wearing an apron and a white hat.

"Excuse me," said Juan-Jesus to the man. "I am going on a trip of three or four days, and I need some food to take with me. I have three dollars. Do you think you could help me?"

The man took a puff off his cigarette and looked at Juan-Jesus. "Where are you going?" he asked.

"It is very important that I get to Florida. It is a matter of life or death—well, almost, anyway," replied Juan-Jesus.

"Well, *hijo*, you look like you could use a good meal. Make it four dollars and I'll see what I can find."

Juan-Jesus nodded. "OK, *Senor*, but I must hurry." He dug into his jacket and pulled out the crumpled dollar bills the waitress had given him. He carefully counted four of them and handed them quickly to the man. The man flipped his cigarette away, took the money, and stuffed it in his pocket. Then he disappeared into the kitchen.

"Please, Lord, don't let this man cheat me," prayed Juan-Jesus.

The man was gone for what seemed like an eternity, but just about the time Juan-Jesus was starting to give up hope, he appeared with two large brown bags.

"Vaya con Dios, hijo," said the man as he gave them to Juan-Jesus.

The bags were heavy, and Juan-Jesus muttered a heart-felt *"Gracias,"* as he scurried back to the parking lot. He looked around cautiously and seeing no one swiftly picked the lock on the side door again. He put the bags inside, crawled in, and shut the door behind him. The inside of the trailer was very dark, but as his eyes adjusted he could see a little patch of light through the vent in the front of the trailer. He put his bags up on the pile of canvas and crawled up on the soft material. There was plenty of room for his small body, and he could even sit up as he went through the bags. One of them contained something warm, and when he looked inside he realized it was a whole roasted chicken with some tortillas and carrots and apples and fruit. He tore a leg off the chicken and bowed his head in the darkness.

"Gloria a Dios, you answer my prayer! Gracias, Padre. I got lots of bread now," he said out loud.

Tyrone pushed the plate of congealed gravy away and attacked the cherry pie and ice cream. He shoveled it down in large bites followed by gulps of coffee.

Man, will I be glad to get home, he thought. The last six weeks had been cheap motels, bad food, endless shopping centers, and pure loneliness. When Orly had asked him if he wanted to make some extra bucks towing the show car around, he had jumped at the chance. He'd been looking forward to being on the open road, taking care of himself, and answering to nobody but the schedule. Initially it wasn't too bad. All he had to do was show up at designated shopping centers and grand openings of one kind or another, roll the show car out of the trailer, and let the yokels gawk at a genuine Winston Cup car in all its glory. It wasn't really a race car. It was one of Orly's old race cars that had been reskinned with late-model bodywork. Then it was painted in exactly the same scheme as Orly's Winston Cup cars with his name over the door and all. The motor was just an untuned racing motor that had seen better days, but it sounded impressive with the open headers and made people jump when he racked the throttle. The car always drew a crowd when he fired it up to drive it in or back it out of the trailer. And it made Orly's sponsors happy to have what appeared to be a race car where folks could see it. But after just two weeks Tyrone was really burned out. The last four weeks had seemed like an eternity. The motels all looked the same, the food tasted the same, and even the people gathered around the car in the shopping center parking lots looked the same. This was it, though. He was done. Now it was a straight shot back to Daytona Beach. He would off-load the show car in the spectator area around the Daytona USA display, where it would sit with some of the other drivers' cars, and he would be done. He could go back to his regular job as a mechanic and best-ever jackman for the Orly Mann Racing Team. Bear and the boys would look pretty good.

Tyrone left the waitress a fifty-cent tip, paid his check, picked up a toothpick, and sauntered across the parking lot. It was still early. He would drive a while tonight before he stayed in another cheap motel. Probably one with a direct view of the interstate and a smell that could only be called "essence of disinfectant." *Oh, well, a bed is a bed,* Tyrone thought.

The pit marshal waved the first car in line onto the track, and a cheer went up from the crowd. Orly sat still, in quiet contemplation, waiting his turn. Qualifying was officially under way. The cars were given one lap to build up speed and then would come flying through the tri-oval, trailed by the sound of thundering exhaust, to pick up the green flag and officially start the clock. Then they had two laps to run belly down and flat out before they were given the checkered flag, which signified the end of the qualifying run. As soon as the car flashed across the start-finish line, the next car in line would drop the clutch and accelerate out onto the track. From the outside it looked a little mundane, maybe even boring. Inside the car it was a different story.

Orly reached over and pressed the red button on the steering wheel with his thumb.

"What's it look like, Jimmy?" asked Orly into the built-in microphone in his helmet.

Jimmy, high atop the Winston Tower in the spotters area, was carefully following each car with a powerful set of binoculars. The Winston Tower was the official home of NASCAR at the track and housed the media center and several other essential organizations. The spotters for the teams gathered on the top of the building, which afforded them a bird's-eye view of the proceedings.

"It's picking up some, Orly, especially coming down the back chute. Better watch it going into three," Jimmy answered in his laconic Texas drawl. Jimmy was Orly's spotter and from his perch high in the air could see the whole racetrack. During the race Jimmy's job was to keep track of everything behind, in front of, and around Orly. Jimmy was a jewel of great price. Without him Orly would be sightless. It took every bit of concentration just to keep the car pointed straight, and it was Jimmy's quiet, gentle voice that kept Orly apprised of the big picture. Jimmy was also Bear's eyes in places he could not see and could tell Bear how Orly's car was handling compared to the other drivers. Jimmy was a vital, integral part of the team. He had been with Orly since the short-track days years ago, even before Bear. He knew Orly well. He knew that

43

when Orly was sitting in the race car, he was one of the most focused drivers ever. He also knew from the tone of Orly's voice that he was concerned. No one in their right mind would ever say Orly was scared or nervous, but concerned was a good substitute. And Jimmy knew why.

Running fast at Daytona was all about air. A Winston Cup superspeedway car, in the words of the engineers, was a carefully crafted piece of high-speed machinery designed to slice through the atmosphere with aerodynamic efficiency. Every part of the body was hand built to precise measurements. Seams were carefully matched between fenders, hood, and decklid so that the body looked like a highly polished piece of slippery glass. It was sprayed with high-gloss paint and finished to a satin-smooth surface. It may look like Mom and Pop's car from a distance, but there were many significant differences. There had to be. Mom and Pop didn't fly down the back chute at Daytona at over 200 miles per hour. Fly was the key word. In order to stay hooked to the track, the aerodynamics of the cars needed to be carefully designed. Every car had a five-inch spoiler built transversely across the full width of the decklid. The spoiler stuck up in the air at a precise angle, which was dictated by NASCAR, and it was designed not only to keep the car on the track but to keep it stable as well. The fronts of the cars were designed with a panel that nearly touched the ground to limit the amount of air flowing underneath. The panels were aptly called "air dams." During qualifying the car's grille openings were taped over to keep the air flowing in the right direction. Too much air beneath the car and the front end got light, making the handling go away big time and causing the car to "push" in the corners. Driving a car with major push at Daytona was like trying to throw a 90-mile-per-hour fastball around a corner. Push, in technical terms, was understeer. In other words, when the driver turned the wheel to make the car go around the track, the car had a tendency to go straight. Anyone who has ever tried to put on the brakes and turn a corner at slow speed on glare ice knows the feeling. The car just goes straight.

Pushing, though, was only one of the things NASCAR drivers needed to worry about. If the angle on the spoiler on the back of the car was not in keeping with the shocks and springs, the down force was greatly affected and the car wouldn't stay stuck to the racetrack in the corners. Then a driver would tell his crew that the car was loose. A loose condition, which was the opposite of push, meant that the back end of the car wanted to come around in the corner. It's like trying to drive too fast around a corner on a gravel road. Technically, this is called oversteer.

The combinations of shocks, springs, and suspension settings on Winston Cup cars were almost infinite, and every team carried an outrageous number of components to cope with various conditions. Subtle things like track temperature—variables of only a few degrees—or half-pound tire pressure adjustments could change the handling characteristics of the car. Like Bear said, "Racin' ain't exactly an exact science."

Then, of course, the biggest variable of all was a driver's ability to drive and feel what the car was doing so he could confer with the crew chief about what changes to make.

And that was the thing that made Bear and Orly good—they spoke the same language and could communicate.

Qualifying was unique. One car at a time, going as fast as the driver could make it go all by itself. The lower the car was to the ground, the better the airflow over the car and the faster it went. NASCAR had a rule that required cars to be a certain number of inches above the ground. All the competitors knew and followed the rules. One way to make the car lower to the ground "at speed" was to use soft springs and shocks that allowed the car to squat down as the air rushed over it. This also changed the angle on the spoiler so it had less drag and the car could go faster. It worked very well when a car was by itself on the track and the driver could keep it in a straight line. But if the car developed a push or was a tad loose, it could be incredibly dangerous. Daytona sat practically in the Atlantic Ocean, and the wind could be strange, particularly in the afternoon. A sudden gust of wind catching the car as it sailed into or out of the thirty-one-degree banking in a corner could be disastrous. It took skill and incredible nerve to make it work. All the drivers knew this, and that's why the good ones got very quiet and stayed focused during qualifying.

"Who's the fastest so far, Doug?" asked Orly, keying the mike button on the steering wheel with his thumb once again.

Doug Prescott had been waiting for his turn. He knew Orly would be asking that question soon, so he was ready. It was his job. He was young, but he had been around racing most of his life and knew and understood the sport. His dad, Bud, had been around racing most of his life too, and he and Doug joked that racing was in their genes. Doug's mom said it was mostly on their jeans and it looked a lot like grease to her. Doug also understood Orly. Doug had been around Orly since Doug was just a little kid. Jimmy was the eyes of the team, and Doug was the ears. It was his job to keep track of what the other drivers were doing. His position during qualifying was atop the hauler, where he had a good view of the track and the pits as well. He was constantly watching, taking notes, and consulting his custom clipboard with the two built-in stopwatches. Jimmy kept Orly apprised of what was happening directly around him. Doug's job was to give Orly the overall picture.

"Most are in the low to high 90s, Orly. The 7 car is on the pole for now with a 91, but I don't think it's going to stick. A lot of guys are complaining about the wind coming off of two and going into three." Doug said all of this quietly and calmly. Orly insisted that everyone on the radio stay cool and collected. He disliked idle chitchat, and most often his standard reply was two clicks of the mike button, which is what he did now.

It was getting close to Orly's qualifying run, and Bear gave him the sign to start the engine. Orly took a look around inside the car once again. Everything looked OK. He flipped the switch on the fuel pump and ignition, which activated a big red light on the dash. Then he pushed the starter button with his gloved finger. The starter whirred for a couple of seconds, which added another line to Bear's already furrowed brow. Then the engine caught with a roar and settled into a crackling cacophony of sound. The exhaust noise from a stock car was different from any other race car. The dual headers dumped the open exhaust right beneath the driver's door, and the sound resonated through the car's steel body, which added thickness and a tinny reverberation to the sound. It was also incredibly gut-shaking loud.

The car ahead of Orly was just coming off of turn four through the tri-oval to take the checkered flag when the pit marshal gave Orly the go-ahead sign. He carefully eased the car into gear and accelerated onto the racetrack. He was careful as he took the car through the gears. The suspension felt soft and springy and anything but stable at slow speed. The car that had just finished qualifying flashed past him and began to slow as Orly roared down the long, back straightaway. Orly put the car into fourth gear and buried his right foot in the floor, pushing the gas pedal down as far as it would go. For just this occasion Bear had put a very light return spring on the pedal, but Orly pushed it down as hard as he could. Lord willing, he would not lift his foot until he had completed both laps of qualifying and caught the checkered flag. He drove up high on the thirty-one-degree banking into turn one as the car picked up speed and positioned himself to come off of turn two next to the wall. Thirty-one degrees was steep. He could get a little run downhill as he entered the back straight, and it would help him build momentum. It didn't seem like much, but it might make a thousandth or two difference. Orly knew the track surface at Daytona like the back of his hand. This was familiar territory, and every bump and rise in the pavement was like an old friend.

The car felt a little loose at this point, but that was to be expected. It took a restrictor-plate motor nearly two laps to bring the car up to optimum speed, and every trick in the book helped. Orly watched the tachometer as he dropped off turn two and headed down the straight. He couldn't feel any wind, but then he wasn't going fast enough . . . yet. The RPMs were gradually climbing toward the red area of the tach, meaning that the engine was nearing peak efficiency. The name of the game was to be absolutely flat out with nothing in reserve when the flagman waved the green flag to signify the official beginning of his qualifying run.

Orly blasted down the straight and could feel the car hunkering down as he positioned himself for the entrance into turn three. He put the car in the middle of the track as the g-force sucked him into the seat. His hands were firm on the wheel as he let the car drift right up close to the wall in turn four. The car was stable and he held the wheel steady. He flashed by the DAYTONA sign painted on the outside wall and set the car up for the tri-oval section of the track. Orly drew a bead on the flagman as he waved the green flag from his perch above the track.

Jimmy's voice echoed in his ears, "Green flag, Orly."

Orly didn't bother to acknowledge. Every ounce of his concentration was focused on keeping the car as absolutely straight as he could as he blasted into turn one. He kept the car low, almost on the apron, as he entered the corner. By the time he banked off two, his line took him high and he was snuggled up close to the wall. The engine now was running high-pitched and clean. It was like he had broken the sound barrier with the roar of exhaust trailing three car lengths behind him. He came off the corner dead solid perfect and eased his tight grip

49

on the steering wheel as he flew down the chute. So far the wind hadn't been a problem. Orly's calf muscle was beginning to feel the strain of standing on the gas pedal. He relaxed his leg a little without letting up on the gas.

Orly consciously took a few deep breaths as he set up the car for turn three. This was the fun part. Every ounce of his being wanted to lift his foot from the pedal, but he fought the urge and trusted the car and the people who made it work. Besides, if he lifted his foot there was every possibility that he would upset the balance on the car and find himself hugging the wall. He dropped into the corner low once again and used every bit of his experience trying to sense what the car wanted in the way of steering input. He let the car drift up high into turn four and this time was less than a foot from the wall at 190 miles per hour. He could feel the cushion of air compress between the wall and the car and used it to get a little rebound shove off the concrete to increase his speed. Maybe he could pick up another thousandth of a second or so. Once again he flashed across the start-finish line as the starter held the green flag with both hands.

Doug whispered a number in Orly's ear without explanation. The number wasn't exceptional but it was OK. He wasn't going to get on the pole for this one, but if he could just keep this ignorant piece of iron pointed in the right direction for one more lap they would have a decent starting position for Thursday's qualifying race.

As Orly entered turn one Jimmy's voice filled his head.

"The flags are moving, Orly. Watch it."

Jimmy meant that a gust of wind was passing over the track and Orly better be prepared as he came off of turn two. Orly, choosing wisdom over glory, held the car in the middle of the corner and gave himself a little extra room as he exited the turn. It would cost him those two thousandths of a second, and maybe more, but he had no choice. He sensed the wind more than he felt it, and the car gave a gentle nudge to the left. That is, it was gentle to Orly. An ordinary driver would have immediately over-corrected and head-butted the wall, trailing a blazing plume of tire smoke and broken parts. Instead, Orly gently corrected the drift and kept his right foot planted on the floor. No sudden moves with these soft springs and shocks, but no lifting of the accelerator either.

This time Orly put the car as low as he dared entering turn three. The little squiggle coming off of two had probably cost an additional hundredth of a second or so. He needed to make it up. The car sailed up the banking, and Orly could feel the tires starting to build heat and the car just now wanting to push a little. Two more laps and it would be a real problem, but he didn't need two more laps. He needed one more corner and then a checkered flag. As he exited turn four, he was so close to the wall that the crowd stood to its feet and gave him a unanimous, "Ooooohhhh," as his backwash sucked paint chips off the DAYTONA sign.

Orly knew what he was doing and dropped off the corner as smooth as glass. Then boom, he was across the start-finish line with the sound of his exhaust trying to catch him, and it was over. As soon as he crossed the line he lifted his foot from the accelerator and noticed that his calf was trembling.

Doug's voice echoed in his ears once more. "We are twelfth fastest and I think it will hold up, Orly. That's not so bad. It will put us on the third row of the second 125." Orly clicked the mike button twice. He was glad that was over. He hadn't left anything on the table. He got everything out of the car that it had to give, and that was all he could do. Now they could get down to the serious business of real racin'.

Orly took a few deep breaths then pushed the mike button again.

"Hey, Bear, tell the engine guys they did a good job on this motor. It was working. Maybe if we had tuned on the setup a little more we might have done better, but I don't know how. At least we're in the show for now anyways."

"Yeah, I'm happy. I'm real happy you didn't kiss the wall on the last lap and make me work all night fixing a car. I think I saw paint chips fly off when you went by, and it looks like they will have to repaint the sign," Bear replied.

Orly said nothing. Just clicked the mike button twice.

"For waging war you need guidance, and for victory many advisors."

Proverbs 24:6

"Speed at Daytona is relative. But it helps if you have a relative that knows how to build fast motors."

Bear, crew chief for Orly Mann Racing

THE NOISE in the garage area was deafening. Air guns rattled and the tinny sounds of wrenches being dropped on the concrete mixed with the occasional roar of an idling motor. Voices shouted and the place was a sea of motion. Qualifying was over, and Orly's time stuck. Bear and the crew were happy but not satisfied. There was always that certainty that if they had just done a little of this or less of that or maybe just tweaked a little somewhere, the car

53

might have gone just a bit faster. But that was racin' and as Bear says, "Nothin's ever perfect."

Now the real work would start. Immediately after qualifying, the cars were rolled back to the garage stalls and quickly taken apart like large, three-dimensional puzzles. For those safely in the show, it was time to discard the qualifying setup and get down to the serious business of preparing the thing to race. Qualifying was done against the clock with a fragile setup and even more fragile motors. Actual racing required a bulletproof scheme that demanded a different mind-set. The qualifying races were sprints compared to Sunday's race, and those could be slam-bang affairs. The motors had to make power and be reliable too, and the handling had better be stable because they would be swapping paint at 200 miles per hour.

This was also a time for the media. The crews were busy trying to get their work done amidst the various non-combatants hanging around and getting in the way. Microphone cables and big video cameras were a constant hazard. Owners, drivers, and crew chiefs found themselves the subject of scrutiny even in the midst of private conversations.

Orly's car was up on jackstands with the wheels off. Two of the crew members were underneath, pulling out the transmission and rear-end gears. Bear was under the hood with some of the other crew members getting ready to lift the qualifying motor out of the chassis. All around them various teams were doing their own versions of the same dance. Paolo was arranging tools and wiping the grease off his hands in front of the immense tool box when Doug caught up with him. They sidestepped a TV crew that was shooting interiors of the garage area and trying to get background information and interviews for the upcoming races. Paolo casually put his hand on the back of a cameraman, steadying him as he was about to back up and trip over an air hose. The man didn't miss a beat and just kept on shooting. Paolo grinned over at Doug.

"Can you believe this, Doug?" asked Paolo.

"Oh, this ain't nothin'," said Doug, looking around the garage. "Wait till race day or tomorrow even." He changed the subject. "Hey, pardner, what'd you think? We're in the show. One major hurdle crossed, or however they say it," as he threw his arm over Paolo's shoulders in a brotherly gesture.

Paolo arranged the tools, slammed the drawer shut, then grinned back at Doug. "Hey, man, did you see how close Orly came to the wall on the last lap. I thought for sure he was going to lose it. My heart was in my mouth."

"Ain't no big thing, bro'. It's just racin', that's all. Orly knew what he was doing. He always does," responded Doug with a smile. He went on, "So?"

"So what?"

"So what time is she getting in?"

"Come on, Doug, you know exactly what time she gets in. I told you already ten times." Paolo was more excited than he let on. Doug was very much aware of Paolo's excitement, and that's why he was giving him a good-natured ribbing. He could see that there was major chemistry going on between Paolo and Alicia. Paolo might not admit it, but it showed.

Alicia was flying into Orlando from San Francisco this afternoon with her Aunty Grandmother. She was visiting her two other Aunty Grandmothers, but mostly she was helping her Aunty Grandmother from San Francisco fly to Florida. Paolo was supposed to give Alicia a call this evening and maybe, just maybe, they could get together in the next few days. Paolo would be busy but Orlando wasn't all that far away, and the tentative plan was for him and Doug to drive over to see her one evening. For reasons he couldn't fully explain, Paolo was anxious to see Alicia. In his mind he just put it off to being homesick, but he really longed to see her.

At that very moment, Alicia was five miles in the air sitting in the middle seat of an overcrowded airliner. Her slim body was wedged between a portly man on her left and Aunty Grandmother on her right. She was anxious to see Paolo, but in the meantime she was just hoping that this interminable flight would end. Aunty Grandmother had incessantly complained about virtually everything for the past seven hours. Nothing seemed to satisfy her, and now she had the window shade pulled down because the pilot was flying too high for her comfort and it made her nervous to look down on the whole world like this, and didn't it seem that they were traveling much too fast? Besides, everyone knew that an airplane as big and as heavy as surely this one must be couldn't possibly stay in the air. It was unnatural.

All of this was expressed in a constant stream of Mandarin Chinese sing-song tone by an Asian woman who could have been anywhere from sixty to eighty years old and didn't weigh one hundred pounds dripping wet.

Alicia reached over and patted her Aunty Grandmother on the hand for the twelfth time in the last fifteen minutes.

"It won't be long now, Aunty Grandmother. We should be landing in a few minutes," Alicia said in Chinese.

"I hope so, daughter. This miserable seat has caused irreparable damage to my spine, and I can no longer feel my feet. Besides that, I think the food has poisoned me and I shall probably die in an hour, two at the most." She patted Alicia's hand and went on in Chinese, "I hope my miserable sisters realize the immense effort I am making to come and see them. Why they would move to Florida is beyond the understanding of a reasonable person. Some people are just so ungrateful and inconsiderate of other people." Aunty Grandmother said all of this in a rush as she leaned forward to glare at the large man sitting in the aisle seat next to Alicia. He was asleep with his mouth gaping open as he snored quietly. "But at least I am not sitting next to Gorgon the Whale Man like you, my child. Do you think he cares that he smells so disagreeable?"

"You better be careful—he might speak Mandarin Chinese," said Alicia.

Her Aunty Grandmother said nothing but snorted through her nose.

Ah yes, Aunty Grandmother, thought Alicia. *I can only imagine what it will be like to spend two weeks with three Aunty Grandmothers. The last time you all were together two years ago the complaints never stopped. At least then I was in my own home and could hide in my room for some peace and quiet.*

The old woman finally quit talking and leaned her head back against the seat. She was asleep almost instantly and snoring nearly as loud as the man next to Alicia. Alicia looked at her fondly and stroked her weathered hand. She really did love this very special lady. She might seem tough and difficult to get along with, but she was actually very tenderhearted. She was one of those people who earned her way in life, and that made her very independent.

At one time Aunty Grandmother was one of four sisters who were very close in age. They lived in China, and their parents died when they were young, leaving them no one to rely on but each other. But they were intelligent and frugal and managed to put away enough money so that all four could emigrate to America together. They settled in the Chinatown section of San Francisco and opened a small restaurant. None of them married, but they were exceptionally hardworking and pooled their resources as they lived together. The restaurant prospered and earned a great reputation and popularity. The oldest of the sisters became pregnant and died while giving birth to a baby girl. It was a grievous loss to the sisters. The child lived, and the remaining three sisters took immediate responsibility for raising the child. This child was Alicia's mother. No one ever told Alicia's mother who her father was and it became one of those unspoken family mysteries. Perhaps one day Alicia would hear the whole story.

Alicia's mother was raised to call all three sisters Aunty. Not Aunty One or Aunty Two or Three but simply Aunty. To some it might be confusing, but to Alicia's mother and the sisters it was perfectly logical. Each sister considered herself not a separate entity but an integral part of the whole that was raising Alicia's mother. Alicia's mother grew up deeply immersed in the Chinese culture and dutifully married a young Chinese man from a successful family in Chinatown. The sisters were pleased. They expected Alicia's mother and her new husband to live in Chinatown and ultimately take over the restaurant business. The sisters were fiercely independent and passed on this quality to Alicia's mother. So despite their disappointment, they were not surprised when the young couple decided to go their own way.

Alicia's mother and father were second-generation Chinese, and they understood the necessity of holding fast to family roots, but they also understood the necessity of assimilating into the American culture. They moved out of Chinatown to the avenues in San Francisco, which was tantamount to moving to a foreign country. The Aunty Grandmothers protested, but only for the sake of appearance. They understood the need for change.

After a number of years, Alicia was born and became the only child in the family. The aunties then considered themselves grandmothers, all three of them, and insisted on being called Aunty Grandmother. The love they showered upon Alicia's mother now spilled over to Alicia, and they regarded her with great fondness. Their grandmotherly rights gave them unrestrained opportunity to tell Alicia how to live her life. Of course they seldom agreed with each other, which in turn made Alicia crazy. The real truth was that Alicia loved all three of them very much. They would do anything for her and could refuse her nothing.

Paolo grew up around the grandmothers and respectfully called them Aunty Grandmother in English. When he was little, he used to joke with Alicia about it and said it sure made it easier for him to remember their names. Though they all wanted to be called by the same name, they were as different as night and day. Each one of them had her own unique personality quirks. But one thing they all had in common was that deep down inside they were gentle, loving ladies who doted on their beloved granddaughter.

One day, inexplicably, two of the aunties decided to move to Orlando, Florida, after going there on a vacation and falling in love with the climate and the atmosphere. There was a large Chinese community there, and they fit in very nicely. They were tired of running the restaurant, they explained, and insisted that the third sister come with them. But in her own independence, she refused and kept the restaurant.

That was two years ago, and now she was traveling to Florida to visit her sisters. She did not want to make the journey alone, complaining that her English was not good enough and that it was barbaric to travel alone, so she insisted that Alicia accompany her.

Aunty Grandmother pretended to sleep and pondered her situation. She would be glad to see her sisters, for she loved them dearly. They loved her as well. After their oldest sister died, she had become the oldest and was therefore considered the wisest of the three. She had sent her two sisters to Florida specifically to find a place to settle, and Lord willing, she would not be far behind. Alicia did not know it yet, but her father and mother were also thinking about moving to Florida. Her father was considering a new job possibility, and he would make his decision in the next few weeks. *Alicia can go to college in Florida just as easily as San Francisco,* Aunty Grandmother thought. She studied Alicia through narrow eyes.

Such a pretty girl with her long black hair, beautiful eyes, and a face that smiled easily. *Yes, Alicia, you think that your Aunty Grandmother does not know that you love that big Pally. But I do and so do your other Aunty Grandmothers. He is a good boy, but I wonder if he loves you. Since he has moved to North Carolina you have been very sad. Perhaps if you live in Florida you might see him more often. Too bad he is not Chinese, but if he loves you then I suppose we can get used to him. We have so far and we have known him most of his life. He is almost like a son anyway. He is a good boy, but he worries too much sometimes.* She patted Alicia's hand. *Aiyee, hurry up big airplane, let's get to Florida. I am tired of sitting.*

Juan-Jesus was sitting on a rock behind a Motel 6 somewhere in Arizona, breathing in the cool night air. He was starting to feel better, but it had been touch and go for a while. Initially the trailer seemed like a good idea, but it wasn't long before the constant swaying motion got to Juan-Jesus. After an hour or so he was sorry that he had gorged himself on so much chicken. The chicken plus the onion rings and hamburger he had eaten on an empty stomach earlier were churning in his gut like an old-fashioned washing machine. Finally, after what seemed like days, the truck stopped and Tyrone called it a night. Juan-Jesus was caught off guard and nearly yelled out loud in fright when he heard the key turn in the lock on the side door of the trailer. Tyrone threw open the door, which automatically turned on the light, as he reached in and lifted the lid on the blue ice chest. He muttered out loud, "Sorta smells like chicken in here. I wonder how come?" He didn't answer his own question and instead pulled out a six-pack of beer and peeled a couple of cans out of the plastic loops, closed the lid, and then slammed the door of the trailer. Juan-Jesus offered a prayer of thanks that Tyrone never once looked up, or he might have seen him lying in the overhang. *Thank you, God, the big gringo didn't corner me in this trailer. No telling what would have happened.*

It was late but Juan-Jesus wasn't quite ready to go back to the trailer. He had all day tomorrow to sleep. He unzipped his backpack and pulled the tattered map from the inside pocket. Holding it so he could see in the light from the motel, he studied the lines. He was probably about here, he thought, placing his finger on I-10. *I wonder how long it will take to get to Florida? Only God knows and God will show me what to do once I get there,* "Won't you, Lord Jesus," Juan-Jesus said out loud. The darkness seemed very quiet.

Alicia had just finished washing her hair when the phone rang in the comfortable townhouse of the Aunty Grandmothers. Her heart skipped a beat and she listened as one of the Aunty Grandmothers answered. She thought it was funny that all three of them spoke perfect English but pretended that they didn't. They didn't think she knew how good their English was but she did. She had too much love and respect for them to spoil the game. She also knew they much preferred speaking in Chinese, and though Alicia spoke Chinese very well, sometimes they reverted to a dialect she didn't know when they wanted to talk privately.

Alicia brushed her hair away from her ear with the towel and listened.

"Hello, Pally," said the Aunty Grandmother who answered the phone. "We are fine, Pally, and yes, they got here OK. Sister was not happy with the flight, but then we were not surprised. Yes, she is here. Let me see if I can find her." Then Aunty Grandmother walked into Alicia's bedroom and handed her the cordless phone. "It's Pally for you," she said with a twinkle in her eye.

"Hi, Pally, how are you?" asked Alicia, trying to contain her excitement.

"Alicia, man, oh man, how was it? I've been praying for you all day. I can't imagine what it was like flying with her across country," said Paolo. Paolo knew what it was to put up with Aunty Grandmother. The last time he had seen her in San Francisco she had pinched his cheeks, even though she nearly had to stand on a chair to reach his face. She also told Alicia to tell him that he ate too much and was getting too big. It made him feel seven years old. One of these days he was going to surprise that woman and throw her over his shoulder and carry her around the room. Then maybe she wouldn't pinch his cheeks.

"It was OK, Pally. Not bad really, but you should see my Aunty Grandmothers now. They are so funny when they are together. They talk so fast and all three of them talk at the same time. I can hardly understand what they are talking about. It's good to see them. I forgot how much I missed them, and it seems right to have all three of them together again. They really love each other. You can tell. So how are things with Bear and the team? I saw on TV a little while ago that Orly qualified for the race. Are you guys in good shape?"

"Yeah, we'll be OK. Bear was pretty worried, but now that we're in he's mellowed some. He and Orly really want to win the Daytona 500 and get the monkey off their backs . . . but then everybody wants to win I guess.

"I'm having so much fun, Alicia, and I'm learning so much. I can't believe I'm really doing this. The only bad part is that I'm missing my friends."

"Do you mean you're missing me, Pally? You can say it. I won't tell anybody."

"Yeah, Alicia, I miss you a lot. So tell me what's going on back home."

They talked for over an hour, and Paolo found himself sharing things with Alicia about his feelings and his fear of making a mistake and all. She was so easy to talk to and besides that, she was incredibly encouraging too. Growing up she had always been his staunchest defender and greatest encourager. He didn't realize it, but she felt exactly the same way about him.

"Yeah, tomorrow we dial in the car with the race setup and get ready for the 125 on Thursday. They close the garage at five o'clock so Doug and me ought to get loose right after that. We could probably get there about 7:30 or so. OK? Do you think that would work?" asked Paolo.

"Sounds good, Pally. I'll be looking for you. Call me if anything changes."

"Hey, Alicia, how is the youth group doing at our church? I bet the Mexicali Team is running flat out with training right now. Boy, it sure feels weird not being a part of that after all these years."

"Yeah, I know, Pally. Me too. They are working hard and Pastor Tom was making the usual appeal for translators. I was thinking of going, but my school schedule is different and I can't afford to miss that many classes." Alicia had a gift for languages and spoke excellent Spanish along with Chinese. She could even talk a little Portuguese with Paolo's dad.

Paolo and Alicia attended an evangelical church in San Francisco, and every spring their high school youth group took part in an outreach across the border in Mexico's Mexicali Valley region. Paolo and Alicia were no longer in the youth group, but for five years they had given up their spring vacation to work with the kids in the Mexicali Valley. It was one of the things that had motivated Alicia to learn Spanish. The ministry had had an impact on both of them and had taught them about reaching out to people who were less fortunate. Through the years they had made many friends in the valley. Pastor Rojas was especially dear to them both. Paolo was proud that he had helped lay the concrete for the floor in the little *iglesia* and he also had driven a lot of nails shingling the roof. Pastor Rojas was a kind older man who worked hard to feed the Word of God to his little flock. The Mexicali ministry wasn't easy and required several weeks of training, but the group's efforts in work projects and backyard Bible clubs gave them a great bond with the Mexican people.

Paolo and Alicia talked some more and then reluctantly said good-bye.

"It's good to hear your voice, Alicia. I guess I'm not afraid to say that I really have missed you a bunch."

"I've missed you a bunch too, Pally. It'll be fun to see you tomorrow night. Say hello to Doug and Bear and the guys for me."

"I'll do that. Bear was asking me about you the other day. Gotta go. See you tomorrow night."

After he hung up the phone, Paolo sat in the crew's motor home and thought for a few minutes. Alicia sounded good. He wasn't homesick. That is, he wasn't missing the folks too much or San Francisco—he was having so much fun. But he sure was missing Alicia. His reverie was interrupted when Doug came out of the bathroom with a towel around his neck.

"So, we all set?" Doug asked.

"Yeah, think so. I got directions and everything," said Paolo with a faraway look in his eye.

"Hey, bro', you know I could stay home if you want. Would give you two some time alone."

Paolo looked up sharply. "No. No, I want you to come, Doug. Alicia is looking forward to seeing you again. We're just good friends, that's all."

Tyrone checked into yet another cheap motel and tried to settle in for the night. He dozed a while with the drone of the TV in the background, and he tossed and turned trying to get comfortable on the sagging bed. Finally he gave up trying to sleep and threw back the covers around two in the morning. He still had a lot of driving ahead of him, and if he couldn't sleep he might as well hit the road. If he left now and drove the rest of the night, he could make some good time. The team needed him at Daytona and the sooner he got there, the better it would be.

🏁

Juan-Jesus was in such despair he was moaning and his legs were trembling. He had made a terrible mistake, and now he stood on the curb by the motel and watched the show-car rig pull away. He couldn't believe his eyes.

Yesterday had gone quickly, and Juan-Jesus could tell Tyrone was in a hurry to get to Florida. It seemed that they were really traveling fast. Juan-Jesus finally adjusted to the motion of the trailer and was doing OK. He was a little bored in the trailer and had even climbed into the car and sat in the bucket seat pretending that he was driving. Last night Tyrone had finally stopped late and Juan-Jesus thought they were probably in Texas somewhere.

After he was sure Tyrone was in bed, Juan-Jesus had crept out of the trailer to look for food and move around a little. His supplies were running low and he at least needed to fill his water bottles. He finally found an all-night gas station and grocery store after walking several blocks and managed to get what he needed. It was dark and late and he had gotten lost trying to get back to the motel. Finally he got his bearings and located the place. Just as he was walking into the parking lot he saw Tyrone pull away. Since it was a balmy evening, he had left both his jacket and his backpack in the trailer. Fortunately he had the little case of lock picks and key blanks in his pocket, but everything else he owned was heading out of the parking lot. He couldn't believe his eyes and almost yelled out for Tyrone to stop . . . but he couldn't do that.

Juan-Jesus frantically prayed as a wave of anxiety rolled over him, "Lord, please, you gotta help me. Please, Lord, don't leave me here in the dark without my things. Please, Lord." He stood staring at the disappearing rig, unable to move.

Tyrone was just about to pull onto the Interstate when he realized that he had left his ditty bag in the room. He muttered a curse under his breath and circled the block to come back to the motel. He pulled into the parking lot and left the motor running as he jumped out and ran up the stairs to his room.

Juan-Jesus couldn't believe it when Tyrone pulled back into the parking lot. As soon as Tyrone jumped out of the pickup, Juan-Jesus wasted no time. He forced his para-lyzed body into motion. He quickly picked the lock with shaking fingers and eased himself into the trailer. He was just barely inside the rig when it began to move. Juan-Jesus sat on his makeshift bunk, rocking with the motion of the trailer and clutching his backpack to his thin chest while tears of relief flowed down his cheeks. The next night he got out of the trailer for just a few minutes, and when he did he kept it in sight at all times. Then he spent the night huddled under the tarps . . . hungry.

🏁

It was Wednesday night and Doug and Paolo had indeed managed to get away and were at this very moment sitting in a pizza parlor with Alicia, laughing and enjoying being young. Paolo's cheeks were still sore from being pinched by all three Aunty Grandmothers. Even Doug got a little tweak when he wasn't looking, and the aunties chattered in Chinese about how handsome and young and strong the boys looked. They told Alicia in Chinese that she was very fortunate to be escorted by two such manly men. Then they gave her a lecture about being home early and asked if she had her key and so on. She tossed her long hair with a smile and gave them a wave good-bye as she and Paolo and Doug ran for the door. It was refreshing for all three of them to get out on their own for a while. In just a few minutes they were old friends again, sharing inside jokes and arguing over the radio. They went to a movie first, and in the darkness Alicia reached over and held Paolo's hand.

In the meantime, a tired Tyrone was pulling into Daytona Beach and cruising up Speedway Boulevard toward the racetrack. Juan-Jesus was awake and watchful. He wasn't certain where they were, but he had a sense that they were nearing the end of the journey. The show-car rig had barely stopped for fuel during the last eighteen hours, and Tyrone made do with fast food along the way. Juan-Jesus was out of food, but he still had a little water left. He was as eager as Tyrone to get this trip over with.

Orly, Bear, Jimmy, and Bud Prescott were in council in Orly's motor home just off the pit area. They were talking strategy for tomorrow's race as they sat around the dining table. That is, three of them were sitting. Bear couldn't sit and talk racin' at the same time. He was leaning with his hips pressed against the counter and gesturing as he spoke.

"You know, Orly, judging from our times I think we got a third- or fourth-place car right now. If we go for the win tomorrow, the best we can start on Sunday is third. The two front-row guys stay there no matter where they finish. It's fifty laps, and you know it gets wild and woolly out there, because a lot of those guys ain't gonna make the main show. Of course, it is more than fifty thousand bucks to win the thing, but that's peanuts compared to the big money on Sunday. To win on Sunday is a million plus some change for the winner. I can't believe the total purse is over eight million dollars." Bear finished his observation by folding his arms.

Bear's point was moot, and he knew it when he said it. The Orly Mann Racing Team raced only one way, and that was to win. It wouldn't have mattered if the prize money was only five bucks—they still would race just as hard. That's what the sport was all about. The influence of money—big money—changed things, but when it was all said and done they raced to win. Period.

Bud spoke, "I sure don't like these restrictor-plate races. Shoot fire, the only way you can finish in the top ten is if you buddy up with somebody."

Jimmy chimed in, "I hate this restrictor-plate stuff too. Four races a year, and they probably cost the teams, us included, ten times what the rest of the schedule costs." Jimmy was referring to the fact that restrictor-plate racing was the most dangerous type of racing the Winston Cup teams ran all year. The cars were always running so close together that it was just a matter of time before somebody screwed up big time and crashed, often taking half the field with him. It was called "The Wreck." Everybody referred to it as such, and everybody knew that in every restrictor-plate race it happened. Sometimes it happened more than once. Jimmy was nervous because he had one of the most important jobs on the team—keeping Orly out of The Wreck. It was an important job, and Jimmy took it seriously.

The conversation went on as everybody talked and listened. Orly trusted these men. In fact, he trusted them with his very life. It took teamwork and cooperation to win races, and it took even more teamwork and cooperation to stay healthy in the process.

Finally the meeting broke up and Jimmy and Bud headed off to their own motor home. Bear stayed a minute to talk to Orly.

"Did Tyrone get in yet, Bear?" asked Orly.

"Yeah, he got in about eight o'clock. Said he drove straight through most of the way. I'm having a little trouble with that guy, Orly, but he still is the best jackman around. Come tomorrow we'll need him. I hope he gets up with his head on straight. We won't have to stop for fuel, but if we get a yellow flag early or you cut a tire or something we still could salvage a good enough finish."

"You know, Bear, I would never tell you how to run the crew, but if you want to let him go I'm with you," Orly said while he rubbed his bad leg.

"It's one of those catch-22 things, Orly. The guy is good. He's fast and you know it takes beef to muscle the jack, but the man is such a bigot. I've been thinking on it long and hard, and we'll see what happens. I've been thinking about training Paolo for the job. He's a big kid, and I gotta tell you, he's a lot stronger than he thinks he is. The only problem is that he's pretty young and has zero experience. Daytona isn't the place to experiment. This place is going to take all we got to give and then some, so I think I'll just stick with Tyrone for now."

"I trust you, Bear. You make the call." Orly yawned and stretched. "We'll see you in the morning. Then we'll know what we got to work with in the 125."

Bear headed out the door and waved a silent good-bye.

Orly dozed fitfully and finally got up sometime after 2 A.M. The dim glow of the night-light illuminated the inside of the motor home. Orly hated the dark and always slept with a light on. He lived by himself and besides, it was no one else's business how he lived. He finally gave up trying to sleep and got up and turned on several lights. He debated whether he should make coffee and thought better of it. He might be able to go back to sleep for a while, but if he drank coffee he'd be up the rest of the night for sure. He settled for a cup of herbal tea instead. He sat down in the dining nook, contemplated the wall, and took stock. He looked around at what he could see of the inside of the motor home and shook his head. It was luxurious to say the least. It had every amenity that a person could ask for, including a queen-sized bed and a Jacuzzi. He owned his own airplane and had his pilot's license to fly it when he wanted. He and Bear were co-owners of a racing team that was worth several million dollars. He had sponsor commitments for the whole season, which would pay the bills and the crew and even leave some for him, which meant that any prize money he won would be gravy. The sale of souvenir merchandise bearing his image was bringing in over three million a year, and he channeled that money into several Christian charities. Yeah, he had a lot and he hadn't done badly for a guy who started his career wrenching at the local Chevy dealership for other drivers.

On the other hand, Orly had a lot of responsibilities. The only reason he was successful was that he won a few races here and there. When he stopped winning, the sponsor money would disappear like spit on a griddle. Having his own airplane was a wonderful convenience, but it cost an arm and a leg to maintain. If the truth be known, race cars were nothing but black holes into which people poured lots of time, money, sweat, blood, and tears. Sometimes they made a little back but mostly they didn't. Driving them wasn't easy either. It wasn't anything at all like what people thought it was. It took a lot more courage than most people imagined. Orly looked down at the hand holding the tea cup—it was trembling slightly. *Man, I hate restrictor-plate races,* he thought. He reached over the back of the couch to the bookcase and brought the worn leather Bible to the table. "Lord, let's see what you have to say to a fearful man who must do battle in the all-too-soon morning."

A fool gives full vent to his anger, but a wise man keeps himself under control.

Proverbs 29:11

"I learned a lot today. If I told you what I learned I'd be telling everybody else what I learned . . . and I'm not going to help them any."

Tony Stewart, rookie Winston Cup driver

THURSDAY MORNING DAWNED slightly overcast with a gentle breeze that barely ruffled the multitude of flags around the speedway. The forecast was for the morning clouds to burn off, and then the air would be clear and bright by race time. Even though it was barely dawn, the parking lots were beginning to fill up. Many folks had slept in their cars waiting for the gates to open. And now that the sun was coming up, people were stretching and yawning as they gathered their stuff for a full day in the grandstands and infield. Just the two Gatorade 125-mile qualifying races would be run this day, but the atmosphere was festive and expectant, and virtually everyone was wear-

74

ing some sort of apparel that announced their preference in teams and drivers. Just two, fifty-lap sprints. Twenty-eight cars in each race with a total purse for the winner somewhere around fifty thousand bucks. Twenty-eight cars in each race—a total of fifty-six cars. Considering that only forty-three would start Sunday's race for the big money, the racing would be hot and heavy.

The 125 races set the pace for Sunday's race, and they were the first event of the long season. Now would be the time to find out whether the testing and hard work during the short, two-month off-season would pay off. The fans were eager and so were the drivers and crews. The off-season had been too long, and it was time to "let the big dogs run," as one popular T-shirt logo put it. It would be hours before anything got under way, but to the thousands of people gathered to watch, it made no difference. They were inside the Daytona International Speedway where the racing was the finest and tightest in the world. These fans were here to witness every bit of the drama. As a result, no one paid much attention to the small Hispanic boy wandering in the midst of the crowd.

Juan-Jesus was lost yet again, and now he was confused. He wasn't sure which way to go, and he was so tired he could barely move. Last night had nearly been the fulfillment of his worst nightmare, and every time he thought about it he shuddered. Tyrone didn't waste any time and, except for a brief stop on I–10 for a short conversation with a Louisiana state trooper, he hardly stopped. Juan-Jesus sat still as a mouse in the trailer while the blue bubblegum flash swept over the rig. He was terrified and thought maybe the *policia* might make the gringo open the trailer. Fortunately his fears were groundless, and the policeman let Tyrone go with a warning.

Tyrone hit Jacksonville and headed south and didn't stop till he hit the speedway. He fought the late evening traffic, was waved through the security gate, and headed straight over to the huge Daytona USA compound to unload the car.

Juan-Jesus sensed that he might be at the end of his journey, and his heart jumped when he realized that they were in Florida. Perhaps he had actually made it. But then without warning the truck stopped, and before Juan-Jesus could react the ramp dropped down at the end of the trailer with a bang, leaving Juan-Jesus blinking in the sudden light, faced by two very surprised men. He was caught like a deer in a poacher's light and sat still, blinking his eyes. One man yelled, "Hey, Tyrone, looks like you got a stowaway here," as he shined his flashlight over the show car and onto Juan-Jesus sitting on the edge of the overhang. Juan-Jesus had no idea what the men were saying, but he knew it couldn't be good. He sat paralyzed with fright.

Then Tyrone came around the back of the trailer. He peered at Juan-Jesus for a minute, then roared, "Hey, I know you! You're that little greaser kid that hit me up for money back in California. What're you doing back there? You wait till I get my hands on you, you little turkey. You better not have hurt this here car, boy. You sit right there; I'm gonna get a piece of your hide." Tyrone followed this outburst with a few well-chosen expletives as he wriggled between the side of the car and the trailer.

As he forced his big body toward the overhang of the trailer, with his arms extended and shoulders hunched, he looked like a WCW wrestler getting ready to body-slam an opponent. Juan-Jesus couldn't take it. He panicked. His eyes were still blinded by the light, but he could see enough to recognize Tyrone's bulky outline, and it was too much for his overloaded senses to handle. He dropped off the overhang and raced down the other side of the show car, running for his very life. With his short stature and thin body, he barely broke stride running out of the trailer next to the car. The men at the back didn't try to catch him. They just stood and watched. It was Tyrone's business and none of theirs. In fact, they laughed uproariously as Tyrone tried to turn around and banged his knees in the process cursing furiously.

Juan-Jesus fled into the darkness, running blindly, crashing through the crowds of people. Several turned to look but no one gave chase. Too late, he realized that he had left his backpack and jacket in the overhang. Now he had nothing. He slapped his pants pockets. Yes, he still had his father's lock picks, but what good were they now? He ran until he was out of breath and could run no more. Finally he found himself next to a cyclone fence that butted into a building, and he wedged himself into the corner and sat down on his haunches. His heart was racing and hot tears were flooding down his cheeks. The events of the past few days were so overwhelming that he couldn't think or even pray. Gradually his heart slowed and the tears dried on his dirty face. Hoping he was safe, at least for the moment, he stayed as still as possible in the darkness.

He sat for perhaps an hour, maybe two. He was in shock and, for the moment, time had no meaning. He was thirteen and in a strange country that he knew nothing about.

He was hungry and tired and he missed his mama and his sisters. Somehow his quest was out of control and not going the way he had imagined it would. He was scared—even more scared than he had been in the desert. He sat quiet, mute with fear. Finally, when the ground got so hard that his hips ached, he got up and began to walk. There were groups of people all walking in the same direction, and unconsciously he found himself following along. He couldn't understand most of what the people were saying, but in his heart he was desperate for human companionship and joined the crowd waiting for the gate to open to the grandstands and infield area of the speedway. In his delirium Juan-Jesus saw himself as part of the family groups that were going somewhere. He pretended that he was with his papa and mama and sisters and that they were going to the circus perhaps. They had gone a couple of times in the plaza back in Mexicali. Maybe later they would eat cotton candy and popcorn.

As the crowd passed through the turnstiles, the ticket takers collected their stubs and gave directions. Perhaps it was because he was little, ragged, and looked inconsequential that no one paid him any attention. Or perhaps it was because the Lord was in control and blinded the ticket takers' eyes. At any rate, not knowing any better, Juan-Jesus followed the crowd into the track.

Paolo was experiencing more feelings than he thought possible. He and Doug had had a wonderful time with Alicia last night. They had laughed and reminisced about the time in San Francisco when Doug had come out to Sears

Point with Orly's team. It was easy camaraderie. Even the movie wasn't half bad. As a result, they headed back to Daytona late. No telling what time it was when Paolo and Doug wandered into the motor home compound and crept into bed. Bear's snoring didn't keep them awake long, but then, in what seemed like ten minutes, Bear was rolling everyone out of bed with boisterous shakes and prods. Paolo looked at his watch and it read 5:30 A.M. He groaned and pulled the covers over his head.

Bear yelled at him and Doug, "Come on, you lazy good for nothin's. It's time to get moving. We got some racin' to do today. I want you boys up and at 'em. The garage opens at 7 A.M. and I want you guys fed and watered with your hair slicked down looking sharp." Paolo looked across at Doug in one of the other bunks and smiled. Doug gave him a grin and a thumbs-up. Yup, Bear was ready to go racin'.

A half hour later, the whole crew was gathered between two motor homes, wolfing down breakfast as Bear went through the strategy for the 125 race. Once the team got into the garage area it would be difficult to get everyone together. This way they could start the day on the same page. It was standard prerace strategy, and they would meet again like this on Sunday morning.

Bear spoke, "OK, everybody listen up. As you can see, Tyrone finally condescended to ease in from the West Coast to come to work and push the jack handle for us. Rumor has it that he didn't come alone."

Everyone laughed because they all had heard about Tyrone's stowaway. Tyrone didn't think it was funny and glared around the group, but no one paid much attention. Bear continued his instructions, much like a football coach dealing with a veteran team that was well prepared for a play-off game. They knew what to expect, and all of them were experienced professionals.

"Now you know they call you 'over the wall guys' the Thunderfoot Ballet Company, and I expect you to do us proud. My hope is that we don't need your expertise, being as how this here race is only fifty laps. But just in case we have to change a tire, I want you to be ready. You know we got the best and most savvy driver in the business, so let's not let him down."

Bear went on. "We need everyone to do their jobs, so let's stay sharp today." There was muttered assent.

The meeting broke up and the guys started heading for the garage area. Paolo stayed behind with Doug for a minute to meet Tyrone. Tyrone was involved in a conversation with another crewman and was saying as Paolo walked up, "Yeah, I don't know how the little twerp did it, but he managed to get in the trailer somehow. He left a worn-out backpack and a jacket in the trailer. Wasn't much in the backpack. Just odds and ends and some papers and stuff. I got me two bucks and some change out of his jacket though. I tell you, them Mexicans are as thick as fleas in California. It almost makes a guy sick. Everywhere you turn that's all you see . . . Mexicans."

Doug interrupted the conversation.

"Tyrone, I want you to meet the new guy on the team. His name is Paolo, and he joined us while you were in California."

Paolo stuck out his hand, and Tyrone ignored it. He looked Paolo over, taking note of his black curly hair and olive complexion, and said, "You ain't Mexican, are you?"

Paolo, who was nearly as big as Tyrone, flushed a little and set his jaw. "No, I'm not Mexican. I'm mostly Portuguese and my mama is from Armenia." He put his hand down.

Tyrone made no reply as he turned his back and went back to his conversation. Doug was embarrassed, and he and Paolo turned and walked together toward the garage area.

"I'm sorry, Paolo. The guy is a jerk and real ornery. I don't know why Bear keeps him on the team, but he must have some reason. Just ignore him." Paolo nodded, saying nothing. He had met the Tyrone-type before, and bigotry was nothing new.

Unbeknownst to the boys, Bear had watched the whole scene. He shook his head as he too headed for the garage area.

Later on in the morning, Orly was just finishing getting dressed for battle when there was a knock at the door of his motor home. He finished tying the laces on his sneakers and stood up. Later he would put on his fireproof driving shoes, but they weren't made for much walking. He opened the door and his face lit up with pleasure.

"Hey, John, how are you? Good to see you. When did you get in?" asked Orly.

The man at the door was a big man with beefy arms and a receding hairline. His official title was Chaplain, and he traveled as much as he could with the NASCAR circus, performing the duties of a pastor. He and his wife, Martha, had done this for many years and were well respected and liked by most of the racing community. Orly and John were solid friends and enjoyed each other's company very much. In fact, next to Bear, John was perhaps Orly's best friend.

Winston Cup racing was a highly competitive business that involved a lot of money, and it seemed everyone had a secret agenda and their hooks out trying to capture some of the gold. John and Martha had no such agenda and liked Orly and Bear simply for who they were as God's creatures. It was a refreshing relationship for Orly and Bear, and Orly treasured the friendship.

"Oh, we came rumbling in late last night. Rumbling for a fact because I had to stop and fix the muffler on the old motor home. We've been visiting the grandkids and just got back from Texas. You look good, Orly. I saw where you qualified pretty good. How you looking for the 125?" asked John.

"We're OK. The usual stuff, but we got a shot at it, I think. We'll see what God does with us. Man, it's good to see you, John. I'm glad you're here. Come on in and sit down. I got a few minutes before the drivers' meeting," Orly replied.

John came in and sat down. The two men talked as only old friends can and caught up on all the family news. They hadn't seen each other since the season ended at Atlanta last November. Finally, it got to be time for Orly to go. John said, "Let me pray with you, Orly, before you head out." He didn't wait for a reply but simply reached across the table and took Orly's hand. John's hand was callused by numerous steering wheels that had guided race cars for thousands of miles on racetracks across the country. It was also a hand that had reached out to many people in difficult situations and a hand that had clenched other hands in times of great grief.

John prayed in a gentle and even voice, "Lord, we ask that you would watch over my brother Orly. We ask you, Lord, to keep him safe as well as the other drivers who are racing today. Lord, we know that this is not an easy day for Orly, for it is the yearly reminder of great loss, and we just lift him up to you and ask that you touch his heart in a special way this day. We pray these things in Jesus' name. Amen." John finished his prayer with a squeeze of Orly's hand.

"Thanks, John, for coming by." Orly brushed a tear from the corner of his eye. "I miss them a lot."

"I know you do, Orly," said John quietly. "Doesn't seem like seven years, does it?"

"No, it sure doesn't. Seems like just yesterday." Orly blinked his eyes. "Hey, John, I've got to get going. See you after the race." Orly was up and grabbed his helmet bag as he headed out the door for the drivers' meeting.

As he left the compound and headed for the garage area, he was mentally trying to shift gears and get his game face on. A man had to stay focused at 200 miles per hour surrounded by a group of people that would like nothing better than to get by him any way they could. It wasn't the time to get teary eyed and reflective. He swallowed the lump in his throat and autographed a program that was thrust in front of him.

The race was a disaster from the "git-go," as Bear would say. Even the best teams have off days, and the Orly Mann Racing Team was no exception.

Orly was in the first 125 because of his qualifying position, and his strategy was simple. He was going to stay as close to the front as he possibly could, and if the opportunity presented itself he would go for the win. If it didn't, he would ride it out and do his best to keep the car out of trouble. At the end of the race, they would have some more input on what worked and what didn't in regard to setup, which would give them a better shot at the big money on Sunday. Winning would be nice, and he was going to do everything possible to make it happen. The main thing, though, was to stay out of trouble and keep the car in one piece. Orly's starting position in the third row was pretty good. The big trouble usually was toward the middle and back of the pack. Those were the guys who had to race themselves into the 500. A fourteenth finishing spot or better guaranteed a chance to run on Sunday. If Orly could stay hooked up with the front draft, he would be in good shape.

As Bear looked over the qualifying sheet, he saw that more than the usual number of big-name, highly sponsored drivers were way back in the pack. There would be some serious racing going on behind Orly. These guys had a lot to lose if they didn't make the race. It was one thing to have a big-money sponsor to pay the bills, but if a team didn't make the most important race of the year it could spell big trouble. Sponsors wanted visibility and TV time. This was why they spent the money to see their name plastered all over a race car. Visibility sold product, whether it was beer or laundry soap, and visibility came to those who could run up front.

Orly's sponsor was a major oil company that had been with him for many years. He knew the management and publicity teams and worked well with them and was a great spokesman for their product. But Orly had no illusions. Lose a few races and start falling down the list of the points leaders, and it wouldn't be long before they would be asking questions and evaluating their commitment. There were any number of guys who would jump at the chance of bagging Orly's sponsor. The company fielded several proposals a year from other teams who felt they could do a better job. So far, the company had been loyal to Orly, and he appreciated it and did his best to keep them happy. A win at Daytona would put a smile on everybody's face. Even a 125 win was nothing to sneeze at. If Orly could win the 125, it would guarantee a second-row starting spot, and that would be plenty OK with everybody as well.

As soon as Orly pulled on the track and followed the pace car, he knew something was not right. He keyed the mike.

"Bear, what the heck is going on? I've got a tremendous vibration in the rear end somewhere. Feels like something is loose back there. I'm coming in."

Bear practically jumped straight into the air at the sound of Orly's voice. Then he felt his stomach sink. He quickly gave Orly a "10-4" and then turned to the crew. They had heard Orly's report through their headsets and were all staring at Bear with big eyes.

"Don't just stand there, Tyrone. Get the jack. Bud, you go under on the right and I'll go under on the left and see what we got. One of you guys throw a jackstand under the thing in case the jack fails. Let's don't panic. Maybe it's something we can fix in a hot minute. Here he comes. Get ready."

Orly, in the meantime, had fallen out of line and pulled down to the inside of the racetrack. He didn't want to push the car too hard, because he might do more damage to whatever was wrong, but at the same time he was desperate to get to the pit lane. He could see the rest of the pack pulling away from him and disappearing into the tri-oval. They would have one more pace lap before the green flag fell and the race was on. The pace laps didn't count. If they could quickly fix what was wrong, he would still be able to start the race on the lead lap. He would have his work cut out for him because now, even in the best-case scenario, he would have to work his way through the rest of the field.

Finally the pit lane came into view, and Orly brought the car down at the mandated speed of 55 miles per hour. He slid to a stop and the crew was over the wall in a fluid motion—that is, everyone except Tyrone. He had inadvertently hooked his foot in an air hose and now fell, sprawling on the inside of the pit wall, dropping the jack. The more he tried to kick free, the more entangled he became. Paolo was standing next to the tool box when he saw Tyrone go down. Bud and Bear were already slithering under the car, and the jack was lying by itself on pit road. Paolo, knowing full well what needed to be done, stepped around Tyrone, went over the wall, and in one fluid motion picked up the jack and slid it under the car. With one quick stroke, the car was in the air.

Bud and Bear both saw the loose bolt on the track bar at the same time. The bolt had not come out yet, but it would have very soon under racing conditions. Theoretically, it couldn't come out because it was supposed to be safety wired, but somebody had screwed up big time. Not only was the bolt not wired, it hadn't been torqued either. Bear slapped a wrench on it and cranked it down tight as Bud held it in place. A quick twist and the safety wire was locked into place.

Paolo watched carefully until Bud and Bear came sliding out from under the back of the car. Then Bobby, the rear-tire changer, jerked the jackstand out and Paolo dropped the jack. It was Orly's sign to go and he accelerated out of the pits in a blaze of tire smoke.

Orly keyed the mike as he took the car through the gears, building speed. "Talk to me, Bear."

Bear dusted the seat of his pants and smoothed his hair before replying to Orly. He didn't want to upset Orly any more than he already was, but he had to tell him the truth, and that wasn't easy. If the track bar had come loose at the wrong time, Orly could have been hurt, or even worse.

"Uh, Orly, somebody left something loose, but we got it fixed. Everything is OK now." Bear wasn't about to tell the whole world over the radio that his team had screwed up big time. He would tell Orly after the race. In fact he knew exactly who had screwed up, and he also had some other business to do after the race, and it wouldn't be pleasant.

Paolo was back over the wall, and no sooner had he set the jack down than Tyrone was in his face with his finger poking his chest.

"Listen to me, you two-bit punk kid. Who do you think you are making a fool out of me? What did you do—trip me on purpose?" Tyrone accented each phrase with a vigorous poke in Paolo's chest.

Paolo said nothing at first, as the color rose up his cheeks. He was suddenly aware that he was looking directly into Tyrone's eyes and that the two of them were almost equal in height. Paolo felt a knot of fear in his belly but swallowed it down and uttered a silent prayer. "Lord Jesus, give me your strength here. I'm not certain what I should do. Maybe I should bust this cracker redneck right straight in the chops." Paolo slapped Tyrone's finger from his chest with a quick, violent motion. Tyrone stepped back, balling his fists.

He looked like he was getting ready to swing when suddenly Bud grabbed him by the shoulders and spun him around. "That's it, Tyrone. What's the matter with you anyway? Come on, we got a race to run. We'll settle this afterwards." Bud said all of this while shoving Tyrone away from Paolo. Then he turned to Paolo. "Settle down, Paolo. Get a hold of yourself."

Paolo stood his ground but he felt shaky inside and slightly sick.

The pit area at Daytona was public domain for the media. No one noticed that every move made by the Orly Mann Team was recorded by the network camera crews. The announcers in the press box were having a heyday trying to interpret the action, but fortunately the comments were short-lived as the pack came thundering down for the green flag.

Orly was still a half lap behind the last-place car when the green flag was waved. Bear, who was unaware of the confrontation between Tyrone and Paolo, spoke softly in his mouthpiece to Orly.

"Howzit feel, Orly?"

Orly was trying hard not to show it, but he was peeved. Somebody had screwed up big time, and it could have cost him dearly. Though he was trying to get his emotions under control, it was no easy task.

"I think it's OK, Bear. But you know I'm no good unless I got a dancing partner. I'm just going to keep my foot to the floor and see what happens. It's already starting to push a little."

At speed, the cars created a flow of air much like the wake of a boat, which meant that there was a calm area directly behind the car. When two or even three cars got together and disciplined themselves to run nose to tail within inches of each other, they could run significantly faster than a single car by itself. It was one of those anomalies of Winston Cup racing that men who were trying to beat one another in the race must cooperate to stay ahead of other competitors.

Orly was in a no-win situation. He could run as hard as possible, but he would steadily lose ground on the rest of the pack. He could do nothing because, as he told Bear, he had no dancing partner.

From his perch in the spotters' area high atop the Winston tower, Jimmy watched the whole situation unfold in the pits through his high-powered binoculars. He was well aware that the TV crew had filmed the whole sequence, including Tyrone's pratfall and Paolo's quick thinking. Jimmy knew there would be trouble as soon as this thing was over. Now what they needed was a quick caution so Orly could catch the pack and at least get in the hunt for a solid finish.

"Give me a differential, Doug. Are they catching me?" Orly's voice crackled in everyone's ear. Doug was perched on top of the hauler with his computer and his stopwatches. He swallowed hard. The news wasn't good. The lead pack was running Orly down at a little over three quarters of a second per lap. Didn't sound like much, but they were running nearly 2 miles per hour faster than Orly. Yeah, they were catching him and doing it quickly.

"Yeah, Orly, they're coming up on you. They'll be on you in about six more laps if it stays green."

Jimmy chimed in. "So far, Orly, the first eleven cars are running nose to tail. Not much racing going on yet. Just keep your foot down."

The mike clicked twice. Then Orly spoke again. "Bear, I'm starting to get a major push going into the corner. I can keep it low so it's OK for now, but as soon as we get a yellow I need some help."

"We'll fix it, Orly," said Bear.

But the yellow never came until it was too late. Orly watched the lead pack come up in his rearview mirror, and then they were on his back bumper. He was tempted to pull over and let them go by, but to do so would put him a lap down, and he more than likely wouldn't be able to get it back in such a short race. As the leaders came up, Orly drifted up the racetrack in front of the leader and allowed him to tuck in behind. Orly could feel the immediate change in the car as it picked up speed. With the other cars behind him, the push was negated to an extent, and Orly found himself enjoying this position. It would have been great if he were leading, but he wasn't. He was the last car on the lead lap, and once they went by him it would be over.

He held the point for three laps, and then the whole group decided that they had enough of following the leader. Three cars pulled out at once, and now they were running two abreast through the corner. In the process Orly got passed and shuffled back to sixth or seventh place. He tucked in behind another Chevrolet and together they drafted back toward the front. This was restrictor-plate racing at its finest . . . and its worst. Now there were fourteen cars all running nose to tail and side by side. None of them were more than three feet apart, and they were running in excess of 200 miles per hour. Orly was so focused he was barely breathing. The cars at this speed and in this proximity were anything but stable. The airflow was all over the place, and it was as if fourteen speedboats were within inches of each other, racing across several riptides. Orly made unconscious, nanosecond adjustments to the steering wheel to keep the car pointed in the right direction, while holding his foot to the floor.

Both Bear and Jimmy had the same thought. These guys were pushing it as hard as they could, and it was only a matter of time before somebody lost it and got into somebody else, which would set off the biggest chain reaction mother of all wrecks.

Jimmy cleared his throat and keyed the mike. "Watch yourself, Orly. It's getting tight." As he spoke the third-place car, which was leading the race a minute earlier, got tapped coming off of turn four. Perhaps it was a simple misjudgment or an errant gust of air, but the consequences were awesome. The car jumped sideways and hit the wall in a cloud of tire smoke. It came back across the track to collect three other cars in the process. This created more tire smoke, and cars that were designed to run in a straight line now found themselves sliding into each other backward and sideways. Debris and the lifeblood fluid of oil and coolant drenched the racetrack, and gobs of screeching tire smoke wiped out visibility.

Orly's vision disappeared in acrid white smoke and what seemed like a bucket of oil slammed into his windshield. He lifted his foot and hit the brakes, knowing full well that it was a waste of effort. He felt the car get loose in the wet stuff on the track and swap ends. He felt the car start to lift then the roof flaps popped open with a loud "thwack." The car settled back down on its wheels, and Orly pumped the brakes with both feet in a useless gesture. Then wham, he was in the wall backward and, just as quickly, rebounded back across the track. He hunkered down as low in the seat as he could and let go of the steering wheel. No sense in breaking a wrist too. He held onto the seat for the ride. He wasn't in control now. He was simply a passenger in the midst of a mad world of sliding and crashing race cars.

Just when things started slowing down, he heard Jimmy's voice in his ear. "Hang on, Orly, it ain't over . . ." The rest was lost in a loud, crackling boom as his car was violently slewed sideways by another car on its side. The bottom of the car slid over the driver's side of Orly's car, showering him with hot oil through his window net. Finally the car slid off and the two cars came to rest against the wall. Orly's ears were ringing as he took quick stock. He wasn't hurt bad. He might not be hurt at all, but it would take a minute to tell.

The spotters' area turned into a frenzied beehive of activity as the men tried to sort things out for their drivers. The yellow flag was out, and whoever crossed the start-finish line first would be leading the race. Some of the less damaged cars were doing their best to limp across the line before heading to the pits for repairs.

Orly blinked his eyes and shifted his attention to his car. Could he get back in the race? One quick look told him the car was trash. The steering column was bent pretty good, which meant everything up front was shoved around. The whole right side was torn off, and he was wedged up against the wall. The tire smoke was just beginning to clear, and the other car had him pinned pretty good. He dropped his window net, which was a signal to the officials that he was OK, and looked at the car next to him. It was the 27 car, which looked like it had rolled over several times. Then he noticed the smoke. It wasn't the ordinary gray of vaporized coolant or even the darker gray of oil smoke. It was black, and that meant it was serious smoke.

Jimmy was surveying the situation when the spotter for the car next to Orly ran over to him.

"Jimmy, my driver is hurt and can't get the steering wheel off to get out. He says the car is full of fuel and starting to smoke. He can't get the fuel pumps off."

Jimmy nodded and keyed his mike. "Orly, you better get out. The car next to you is full of fuel. He says it's getting ready to torch off. The driver is hurt and can't get out."

Orly didn't bother to respond. He quickly undid his belts and crawled out the window. The safety crews were good—excellent in fact—but in a crash of this magnitude it would take a couple of minutes to get to all the drivers. Orly dropped to the track, being careful not to fall down. Thirty-one degrees of banking was pretty steep. Just as he straightened up, the car next to him erupted into flames with a sudden whoosh. It wasn't supposed to happen with all the safety equipment, but no amount of engineering and fabrication could handle every aspect of a 200-mile-per-hour multicar crash. Gasoline was insidious and could be lethal.

Orly was blown back for a minute with the blast of flame, but then he got his feet under him and ran around to the side of the burning car. Fortunately most of the fire was in the back, and Orly could see the driver holding his broken arm close to his body. He was desperately trying to pop the quick release on the bent steering wheel with his good arm so he could get out of the car. The frame was twisted in such a way that he couldn't get the angle he needed with his good hand. Orly dropped the window net and reached through the window with both hands and popped the steering wheel off. He punched the center release on the safety belts with his gloved fist, and the belts popped loose. The flames were working their way toward the front of the car, and Orly could feel the enormous heat through his gloves and fireproof uniform—a uniform guaranteed to withstand direct flames for about fifteen, maybe twenty seconds. He had to work fast. The other driver turned sideways and pushed himself toward the window, and Orly grabbed him under the shoulders.

Just as Orly pulled him out of the car, they were both showered with foam as the safety crew came running up to help. Eager hands helped Orly pull the man away from the burning car, and then both men were surrounded by rescue personnel. They guided Orly down the banking and into the waiting ambulance. He sat back in the jump seat and started to take his helmet off. In a minute they had the other driver strapped to a gurney and slid him up into the rig. He was lying on his back with his helmet still on. His eyes locked on Orly's face and he gave Orly a quick thumbs-up. Orly patted his shoulder and finished taking his helmet off. It was only then that he realized that when he was splashed with the hot oil he had been singed pretty badly himself.

Lazy hands make a man poor, but diligent hands bring wealth.

Proverbs 10:4

"I like that high groove here. When you hit the wall, you are a lot closer to it, and you don't hit near as hard."

Kenny Schrader, Winston Cup driver, car #33

BEAR WAS WAITING when Orly walked out of the medical care center, and Orly had to stifle a smile. Bear was wringing a red shop towel in his hands, and his eyebrows looked like they were stitched together below his furrowed brow. If worry was wealth, then Bear was a billionaire. There was a mob of media people jockeying for position and waiting to interview Orly and some of the other drivers who had been involved in the crash. Bear pushed his way through the cameras and microphones and stepped through the gate around a security guard into the restricted area behind

95

the fence. He stopped in front of Orly and gave him a critical look. They spoke together quietly.

"Well, that was a real effort, wasn't it. Is the car a write-off? What the heck happened anyway, Bear? Good grief, I can't recall us ever making a mistake that dumb. And was that Paolo working the jack? What in the world happened to Tyrone? I thought for a minute there the jack was coming through the window net inside the car with me."

For the moment Bear ignored the questions. He was still checking his friend over carefully. Satisfied, he said, "You OK, Orly? Did you get burned at all? I ain't seen a fire like that in a while. Let me see your hands." Bear grabbed Orly's hands and turned them over. There were a few bright pink spots on the back where they had been singed, and one hand didn't have any hair on the fingers, but the burns were only superficial. His flameproof gloves had done their job. Orly had another spot down low on his neck where the hot oil had splashed under his helmet and onto his neck, which the doctor had covered with a small bandage. His driver's suit was a wreck and was covered with burned and dark brown singed spots.

"I'm all right, Bear. Dog, what happened?"

"Uh, I don't know how to say this, Orly, but I'm sorry. It had to be my fault. One of the guys left a bolt loose on the track bar, and it wasn't even safety wired. I can't believe somebody didn't see it." Bear threw his hands up in the air, then went on. "Yeah, that was Paolo working the jack. He did OK. In fact, I think he was the only one of the whole crew who understood what was going on. Tyrone had the jack in his hands getting ready to go over the wall, and I guess he got tangled in an air hose. Anyhow, I don't know, because you know we always keep them coiled up nice. At any rate, he took a header and fell flat on his face. They got it on camera, and I'm sure it will be on all the clips on the news. When he fell he flung the jack over the wall, and I'm surprised it didn't land in your lap. Paolo just stepped over, picked it up, and slid it under the car so we could fix the problem. After we got you fixed and out, Tyrone got into Paolo's face pretty good. I guess Bud had to separate them, but from what I understand the kid wasn't going to take any guff from Tyrone. The sad thing is that they got it all on tape. You know how it is—those camera guys are all over the place now. They got the whole thing with Tyrone poking Paolo and whatnot. They're going to want to talk to you about it, I reckon. Just tell them it was a friendly conversation." Bear said this without hardly taking a breath while gesturing with his thumb over his shoulder indicating the waiting media.

"Yeah, I'll talk to them in a minute. How's the car? Probably a write-off. What does this mean for Sunday, I wonder?" asked Orly.

"Oh, it's junk. Both the front and rear clip are honked. We might save some parts, but we definitely are going to have to cut it up and start over, which means we'll have to take a past-champion provisional and start last or close to it. We got the backup, but it ain't a speedway car, and we was hoping to keep it set up for Rockingham next week. We're running behind at the shop with these new rule changes and whatnot. At least we're still in the show. Don't know exactly where we'll start until the other 125 is over, and then they'll sort it all out. It'll be fortieth or below, that's for sure. I think when it was all said and done, sixteen out of the twenty-eight cars was involved in the wreck, but only six couldn't take the restart. The pole sitter won the race finally. What a mess! Don't you just love restrictor-plate racin'?" said Bear, with a disgusted shake of his head.

"Well, we better get loaded up and head over to the shop. Looks like we got some all-night fixing to do," said Orly.

Like many race teams, Orly leased a small shop just outside of Daytona Beach. The teams spent so much time in Florida that it made things easier to have another shop handy rather than drive all the way back to Charlotte. It wasn't nearly as large or well equipped as the big shop, but it would allow them to either fix the wrecked car or prepare the backup without worrying about NASCAR closing the garage at five o'clock and not reopening until seven the next morning. Those were valuable hours, and the garage area was too restricted to accomplish what they needed to get done.

"Yeah, and then we'll have to recertify the car with the NASCAR inspectors, and you know what a pain that will be," said Bear. NASCAR was a stickler for rules. In their eyes it kept the competition even, and they were right. Most of the inspectors were former racers, and they knew most of the cheating tricks as well as the crew chiefs. Before the car could get back on the track, it would have to go through a rigorous inspection. It wasn't just the rules that counted, it was the safety equipment as well. Every bit of the car would be poked and prodded, inspected and certified. When they were satisfied the car would be allowed to race. It was a tough system but it worked, and many a driver owed his physical well-being to NASCAR's tough safety rules.

Orly looked at the press of media on the other side of the fence. "I better go face the mob out here and put the best spin I can on this thing. Man, what a way to start the season," Orly said with an equally disgusted shake of his head. "Hey, Bear, get to the bottom of this, will you? If you need to fire somebody or cut them loose or whatever, do it before somebody, mainly me, gets hurt."

"Yeah, Orly, I will. I already got the boys gathering the stuff. I'll see you over at the shop when you get there."

Orly walked back through the gate into the sea of microphones and cameras. Bear smiled and waved but kept walking. "No time right now, folks. We got a lot of work to do. Gotta get going. I'll speak with you later. Yes, I'm OK. No, it wasn't anything personal. Just a couple of the guys working out a little difference," Orly said as he marched quickly through the crowd.

Paolo could feel Tyrone's hot glare burning the back of his ears as he helped the rest of the guys load the stuff into the hauler. Tyrone kept muttering things under his breath while he looked threateningly at Paolo. Paolo said nothing and continued to work with his head down.

"Paolo, take these two gas cans on the wagon over to Unocal and tell them to credit us," said Bud. Paolo nodded his head and grabbed the handle to pull the specially made wagon with the two bright red eleven-gallon gas cans. Tyrone gave one of the cans a kick and said, "Try not to lose them, Fumbles, and don't let no one take any pictures of that pretty face and curly black hair." Then he laughed, a sound much like a braying donkey.

Paolo swallowed, managed a weak smile, and headed out with the wagon. Once again he said nothing, though he was saying plenty in his mind as his dark face indicated.

Juan-Jesus was wandering aimlessly. He could hear the noise of the race cars, but it held no interest for him. He was lost again, and now he did not even have his meager resources in his backpack or jacket. He was tired—achingly tired—and very hungry. He watched as a man ate half a sandwich and then threw the other half in a trash barrel. He waited until the man left, then fished it out, refusing to think, and quickly ate it without even tasting it. He was in the midst of thousands of people, but never had he felt so alone in his life. His wandering led Juan-Jesus down yet another cyclone fence, and he found himself next to what looked like a lot full of tires. They were stacked four high, and there seemed to be hundreds of them. They were butted up on the inside of the fence, and he was on the outside. But at least they offered a little shade. He sat down with his back to the wire mesh, put his head in his hands, and prayed softly in his native Spanish.

"Lord Jesus, what should I do now? I'm really lost and I'm very scared. Lord, I'm the most scared that I have ever been since I left my mama and sisters. Please, Lord, help me." Those were the only words he could speak and he said them over and over again. "Help me, Lord Jesus, help me."

Then Juan-Jesus stood up and began to walk along the fence with his head down, pulling a Popsicle stick along the mesh. He looked up to his left, inside the enclosure, and blinked his eyes in disbelief. It couldn't be, but maybe it was. He was as big as, if not bigger than, the last time Juan-Jesus had seen him in Mexicali, but there was no mistaking that dark curly hair.

Juan-Jesus turned and grabbed the mesh with both hands and tried to shout, but at first the sound came out of his dry throat as a croak. Finally, he got his voice to work and shouted through the fence.

"Paolo, Señor Paolo. Paolo!" Juan-Jesus shouted as he ran along the fence trying to match the pace of the young man pulling the wagon. He was walking very fast. There were so many people and the noise was so loud. He yelled again, "Señor Paolo," as loud as he possibly could, his voice cracking with the strain, "Paolo, Señor Paolo!"

Paolo too had his head down as he pulled the tire wagon. He had much on his mind with this Tyrone thing and Orly crashing. He was wondering who had left the track bar loose. It wasn't him, because Bear hadn't allowed him under the car unsupervised yet. Probably was Tyrone, although that didn't figure because Tyrone didn't do any of the suspension stuff. He worked with Eddie the gear man on the rear-end gears and transmissions. As he was walking lost in his thoughts, he thought he heard his name. He looked up and looked around. Yeah, somebody was calling his name. He stopped and looked toward the fence and saw a ragged teenage Mexican kid in a dirty T-shirt and worn-out jeans waving at him. He squinted and looked carefully at the kid. It didn't compute. He thought he knew this kid, but that was in Mexicali, Mexico, and this was Daytona Beach, Florida. Besides that, the kid he knew came from the poor side of the canal in Mexicali, and he couldn't possibly be here inside the racetrack. He barely had enough to eat, let alone travel. He squinted again and shook his head. *Nah, couldn't be him,* he thought. He was just about to continue toward the Unocal gas station in the garage area when he heard the kid yell.

"Palito, venga aqui, por favor."

The voice immediately took him back to the Mexicali Valley because it was what the little kids called him. "Palito," which was a play on words, meant "little Paolo," which, of course, he was not. The black-haired, bright-eyed kids would call him that in their high, shrill voices and then laugh uproariously. Then they would beg him to twirl them around and carry them on his shoulders. Paolo stopped in his tracks. He looked, then pulled the wagon up to the fence.

He stared at the dirty, tear-streaked face and asked, "Juan-Jesus, is that you?"

"Si, Señor Paolo, mi amigo, it is me," Juan-Jesus said in a small voice.

Paolo reached through the wire of the fence and pulled Juan-Jesus close to him by his T-shirt and looked into his face. "What in the world are you doing here?" He stared at him intently, "Boy, you look pretty rough. You need a bath and you look like you haven't eaten in a week."

Juan-Jesus nodded his head, smiling. He didn't understand all of what Paolo had said, but now at least he had a friend, and that friend had a grip on him that felt very reassuring.

Paolo knew Juan-Jesus didn't understand him. He searched his mind for the Spanish he knew wasn't there. Five years in a row, twice in some years, he had traveled to the Mexicali Valley with the youth group from his church in San Francisco to help Pastor Rojas with his little evangelical church and small body of believers. Every year he planned on learning more Spanish, but it never happened. But he knew this kid. He had watched him grow up in poverty and squalor along the canal outside the city. Juan-Jesus was just one among the many kids to whom Paolo and his friends had ministered and become attached. For a whole week they would run a daily vacation Bible school where they would play games and do crafts, all the while explaining who Jesus is, mostly through interpreters. The most common language spoken was the language of love as the North American high-schoolers shared their faith with the Mexican children. It was a great time, and many of the young people had pen pals in the Mexicali Valley.

Paolo finally managed to find some of the words and with a mixture of English and Spanish asked Juan-Jesus, "Are you solo . . . let's see . . . man, how do I say this? . . . are you by yourself? No mama or papa? . . . no, that wasn't right." He knew Juan-Jesus's papa had died two years ago. Where was Alicia when he needed her? She spoke Spanish fluently. That was probably why he never learned Spanish. Alicia was always around to translate.

"*Si, Señor Paolo,* jes me myself," said Juan-Jesus. "*Comida, Paolo, por favor.* I *mucho* hungry."

Paolo made a quick decision. Bear would be looking for him to help load the stuff and move the Orly Mann team from the garage area at the track to the shop in town. "You stay here. Right here. You understand? I'll come and get you. Now don't move. OK?"

Juan-Jesus said nothing, just looked at Paolo with big saucer eyes.

Paolo turned his back and quickly pulled the wagon toward the gas station. He had to dump these cans and then figure out what to do. He looked back over his shoulder to see Juan-Jesus plastered against the fence, hanging onto the wire with both hands. Paolo gave him a wave and then hurried as fast as he could.

He almost ran back to the garage area. As he went into the team stall, he saw Bear picking up the last of the stuff. Bear saw Paolo and said, "Paolo, I want you to ride with Jimmy in the hauler over to the shop in case he needs some help getting across town in the traffic or anything. We're just about loaded, so get moving. He's waiting for you in the hauler. The rest of the crew will be there waiting on you both, so don't dawdle. I'm going to ride with the flatbed tow truck driver and get him to drop the wrecked car right in the shop. It'll save us time. We have to assess the damage and see what we got." Bear added, with a slap on Paolo's back, "Come on, boy! Get moving."

Paolo was going to say something but couldn't. He couldn't just tell Bear, "No, I have to take care of something first." So he shut his mouth. Just then Doug came walking up.

"Doug, do you trust me?" asked Paolo.

"Well, that's a silly question. Of course I trust you. Why shouldn't I?" said Doug.

"Doug, I need you to do something, and I don't have time to explain. It's a matter of life and death, I think, and I can't tell you why." Paolo then went on to explain what Juan-Jesus looked like and where he would be waiting.

Doug listened intently to get the details. Then he said, "Uh, Paolo, after I find this kid, what should I do with him? I don't speak Spanish any better than you do. What makes you think he's going to come with me anyway?"

"I'm not sure, Doug, but I think he might be in big trouble, and I bet you he doesn't have a visa, which means he is probably in the country illegally." Paolo stopped speaking for a minute and got a very strange look on his face.

"Doug, did you hear Tyrone and them talking about the Mexican kid that was stowed away in the show-car trailer?"

"Yeah, I heard the story. They said he probably rode all the way from California in the back of the trailer. Be a hard way to travel, I would think."

"Doug, I think this might be the same kid, and he's a friend of mine." Paolo looked over his shoulder and then added, "Please, Doug. We can't just leave him. He's just a kid, and I feel certain he really needs our help. I gotta go; Bear's looking at me."

"I heard you, Paolo. I'll take care of it right now. Get going, and I'll see you at the shop." With this Doug headed toward the pit gate.

Juan-Jesus was holding onto the wire exactly where Paolo had left him. He had not moved an inch and was carefully searching the crowd waiting for Palito to come back. Paolo had disappeared into the crowd, and Juan-Jesus was willing him to return. He looked like a fly stuck in a spider's web as he hung on the fence.

Doug spotted him a long way off and breathed a sigh of relief. He didn't want to have to tell Paolo that he couldn't find the kid. There he was. He sure did look raggedy and a whole bunch scared.

Doug eased up behind Juan-Jesus gently, like he would approach a spooked horse. He smiled and said, "Hi, my name is Doug and you're supposed to come with me."

Juan-Jesus spun around and looked at Doug with fear in his eyes. He was not Paolo and he was not sure what this gringo wanted. Then he looked a little closer and realized that this guy was wearing clothes just like the *mas grande gringo* who had chased him from the trailer. Juan-Jesus shrank back against the fence and looked around, planning his escape. Then he remembered that Palito was wearing exactly the same clothes. *What is going on here, Lord?*

Doug wasn't sure what set him off, but he could see that the kid was terrified. Doug put up both hands with his palms out in the universal gesture of peace.

"Hey, don't get spooked. I'm here to help you." He searched his mind for what to say, then said, "Paolo sent me. Paolo, your friend Paolo. Amigo. You know, Paolo amigo."

The name Paolo sank in with its connection to amigo, and Juan-Jesus relaxed a little. Maybe Paolo had sent this guy. He looked around to see if he could see Paolo, but he was not in sight. Juan-Jesus thought a moment and made up his mind, then gave up and shrugged his shoulders. At least this guy acted like he knew who he was. Somebody was better than nobody.

"OK, I will go," Juan-Jesus said and reached out and took a startled Doug's hand. *I guess I have to trust this guy, Lord,* Juan-Jesus prayed.

For a moment Doug felt foolish holding hands with a small-for-his-age thirteen-year-old Mexican boy, but that feeling quickly passed. It was evident that Juan-Jesus needed help, and Doug suddenly felt very protective. He walked with Juan-Jesus toward the security gate of the pit area. The security guard looked at Doug in his crisp Orly Mann Racing Team uniform and saw the credential in a plastic cover hanging from his belt. He started to say something but thought better of it as Doug gave him a defiant look and continued to hold on to Juan-Jesus's hand, dragging him through the gate. Then Doug smiled a toothy smile at the guard.

"He's our new team mascot. Going to get him fitted with a uniform."

"Yeah, right," the guard said and waved them through the gate.

Doug walked quickly through the garage area, holding tightly to Juan-Jesus's hand, hoping no one from Orly's team would see them. Then just as quickly they headed through the other gate to the motor home compound. That guard didn't even give them a second glance.

Doug was formulating a plan. Right now, Juan-Jesus needed sanctuary, and there was only one place to get it. Doug needed a place to stash him where there would be few, if any, questions, and he also needed a place where someone would give Juan-Jesus something to eat and take care of him for a while. It wouldn't be smart to bring him to the other shop with the whole crew there, especially Tyrone.

He led Juan-Jesus over to an older model motor home that sat like a poor sister among the more luxurious rolling castles of the teams and drivers. There was a small Christian fish sign in the lower corner of the windshield, and lettered over the side door in block letters was this:

Pastor John and Martha
Mobile Chapel—Evangelical Ministries
All Welcome

Underneath lettered in careful script was this:

Jesus says, "Come to me, all you who are weary and bur-
dened, and I will give you rest. Take my yoke upon you and
learn from me, for I am gentle and humble in heart, and
you will find rest for your souls."

Doug knocked on the door, and after a minute it
opened and Martha said, "Hello, Doug. What do you have
there?"

"Hi, Martha. Is Pastor John around?"

"No, he isn't, Doug. He's over at the care center. He'll be
back in a little while. Is there something I can do for you?"

"Oh, boy, I don't know where to start. This guy here is a
friend of Paolo's from Mexico, and we think he might be in
trouble. He doesn't speak much English, and right now we
aren't sure what to do with him. He just showed up at the
track. We need to find somebody who speaks Spanish, but
in the meantime we need to find him a place to stay. You
don't speak Spanish, do you?" asked Doug in a rush.

"No, Doug, I don't speak Spanish. Just a few words here
and there. What kind of trouble do you think he might be
in? He doesn't look very dangerous. In fact, he looks dirty
and hungry."

Juan-Jesus looked back at Martha as she looked at him.
She looks very kind, thought Juan-Jesus. *She looks like a
nice mama who knows how to take care of kids.*

Doug said, "I have to get going. Bear has called a team meeting over at our Daytona shop and I got to get there. Martha, can I leave this kid with you for just a little while? We'll come back for him later. I promise."

"Why, I guess so, Doug. Are his folks around anywhere? Is somebody looking for him?" Martha asked.

"No, we think he's here by himself, and we think, but we aren't sure, that he stowed away in the show-car trailer and rode all the way here from California. At least that's what we think. I don't know, Martha. I just met the kid ten minutes ago. Paolo is the one who knows the details."

Martha could tell from Doug's expression that he really was at a loss. "Sure, we'll take care of him." Saying this, she opened the door wide and invited Juan-Jesus inside the motor home. He liked the look of this nice lady and let go of Doug's hand and went inside.

"Thanks, Martha. We'll be back as soon as we can," Doug said as he retreated back toward the garage area.

A few minutes later, Pastor John opened the door of the motor home and stepped in. He saw Juan-Jesus sitting at the table working his way through an enormous bowl of soup. Juan-Jesus looked up and smiled. Pastor John, with his long years of ministry experience, was used to just about anything.

"Hello, young man. You look like you just blew in with the wind." Pastor John sat down on the cushion opposite Juan-Jesus. "Well, Martha, would you care to fill me in?"

"Be glad to, John, except I don't know anything much. He's hungry, dirty, and looks pretty worn out, and I don't think he speaks much English. He did stop to pray before he dived into the soup, and this is his second bowl. Plus

I think he's drunk about a quart of milk so far. Doug Prescott brought him by like you would a stray puppy and asked if we would keep an eye on him for a little while. That's all I know."

Pastor John simply said, "Oh," as he watched Juan-Jesus polish off the rest of the soup.

Half an hour later Juan-Jesus was freshly bathed and dressed in a pair of Pastor John's pajamas and slippers, which made him look like Bozo the Clown. He didn't care. He had just polished off a large bowl of strawberry ice cream and was now comfortably full. Even though it was early, he was so tired he could hardly sit upright, and his chin kept falling on his chest as his eyelids fluttered. The days and nights in the trailer had been anything but restful, and last night had been like a bad dream. This spot had the feel of a safe place, and as he allowed himself to relax his fatigue was overwhelming. These people were kind and gentle. He desperately needed to sleep and offered no resistance as Pastor John sent him back to the spare bunk. Pastor John held back the covers and Juan-Jesus crawled in and was asleep before John finished gently tucking him in.

Pastor John and Martha stood looking over the young boy, wondering what his story might be. John took Martha's hand, and they quietly prayed over the sleeping boy and left him to his dreams.

🏁🏁

The shop was anything but peaceful. The flatbed tow truck brought the crumpled race car into the bay and gently lowered its remains to the garage floor. It was still trickling a little oil and water from the ruptured radiator and oil cooler. In the meantime Jimmy backed the hauler up to the other door, and the spare car was unloaded by several members of the crew. Twelve guys traveled with the Orly Mann Racing Team, and that included Bear and Orly himself. There was another group of guys back at the main shop in Charlotte, and if need be, Bear could have one or several of them fly in. If push came to shove, they could have them bring a complete car from the shop. Bear had already assessed the damage and figured they could fix what they had with the regular crew. The car was wrecked, but it wasn't as bad as he first thought. Once they got the geometry right and the center chassis squared up, they could piece it back together.

It was now past suppertime, but there would be no rest this night. In fact, supper was on its way from a local restaurant, and most guys would eat with one hand while they worked with the other. They needed to jump on the wrecked car—and fast. The first step was to strip it down completely and cut the wrecked body off. It would take most, if not all, of the night to have it ready for the track tomorrow, Friday. Even though the race wasn't until Sunday, because of the support races practice time would be limited. The Goody's Dash would be run on Friday, and the Busch Grand National race would be run on Saturday.

The team would need every bit of practice to dial in the car and make it competitive for the big race. Race cars were temperamental, and just because they were built alike didn't mean they would handle the same. Each car was unique, and it would take a little while to see what type of personality this one had.

To further complicate matters, starting at the tail end of the pack on Sunday meant a different type of strategy. Orly had the monumental job of working his way through the whole field, which meant that he must do his best to stay out of trouble and be aggressive at the same time. They would have to make some subtle changes on the car. This car would have to be solid in the draft, because Orly had some serious racing to do and would need every ounce of expertise Bear and the boys could give him. Bear would have to make the car handle in the midst of traffic, which meant they would have to change some elements of the aero package. In layman's terms, make the car more stable as Orly worked it through the slipstreams of the other cars. Bear could do it. His engineer's mind was already calculating shock configurations and spring rates. He and Andy, the chassis engineer, had already banged their heads together in a blue haze of computer printouts and practical experience.

But there was other business to take care of first. As soon as the flatbed tow truck driver was gone, Bear called a halt to the activity in the shop and had the doors closed. Orly was not there yet, but that didn't matter. This was Bear's end of the operation and he knew what he was doing. In the eyes of the crew, Orly was the driver, which meant he was "out there" somewhere. They all loved Orly very much and respected him and his ability and would certainly hasten to do anything he asked or needed. But Bear was one of them and could outwork and outthink them all. He was in fact "the Bossman," and everybody knew it. At least most everybody.

The crew gathered around in expectation, and Bear perched himself up on the roof of the wrecked car facing the group. Bud leaned against the crumpled hood beside Bear.

Bear began, "All right, you guys, you know fixing a wrecked race car is nothing new. We can do it and we can do it right. We done it before and we'll do it again. But we got a problem. You see, we shouldn't have had a wrecked race car. We put Orly in a heck of a fix. We had a great starting spot and we were looking good for Sunday, and the next thing you know he is running dead last because of us. Now what I want to know is who left the bolt loose on the trailing arm and didn't safety wire it?" Bear waited what seemed like a long time and then went on.

"Ain't nobody going to 'fess up. Well, I'm glad, and I'll tell you why. This isn't easy for me to say, men, but I'm the one who screwed up. It was me that left it loose, and I admit it." There was an audible sigh in the room as the crew stared at Bear with anxious faces. They knew full well that they had Orly's life in their hands, and this was something that had been eating at every one of them since the race. No one liked to look foolish at any time, but especially not when you had an international audience watching your driver live on a gazillion TVs. But that was secondary to the fact that you might be responsible for him and maybe a bunch of others getting hurt. No crew wanted that kind of reputation. Certain crews in the game had a reputation for carelessness, and they often had trouble keeping a decent driver. It was major embarrassment when your car had a good starting position and then had to hit the pits with a problem that shouldn't have occurred.

Every man on the crew knew exactly what the problem was that brought Orly in the minute Bear and Bud climbed out from under the car, though they did not speak of it even to each other.

Bear continued, "I undid the bolt to make an adjustment, and then I got sidetracked by something else and lost track. I have never done that in my whole life and I will never do that again. I guess the Lord is telling me that I ain't perfect. Now I have to tell my driver that I was the one who started the whole series of events that got him caught up in that wreck. At any rate I'm sorry, and I apologize to you guys as well. It was a dumb mistake, and I guarantee you it won't happen again."

There was a low mutter of approval from the team and a general shuffling of feet and awkward looks. They knew Bear's confession took courage, and many crew chiefs would have found the easiest scapegoat rather than take the blame themselves. Sacrifice of ego was generally not part of the racing game, but Bear was different. And that's why they loved him and worked their tail feathers off for him.

But Bear had a little more to say. "Now that I have said that, we've got some other business to take care of. Somebody, starting with you, Tyrone, tell me what happened when Orly came into the pits."

Paolo felt his stomach drop into his shoes. He was standing in the back of the group, still not certain of his status with the team, and he was doing his best to look invisible. Now several of the fellows turned around and looked at him.

Tyrone was upset. Bear had put him in a place where he had to explain what had happened. If he said he tripped, he would look foolish and it would be a difficult thing to live down. If he said somebody tripped him, there were a number of guys who might say he was lying. Then again, they might not because he was big and strong and could be ornery. But there was another possibility. Tyrone thought maybe he could charm his way out of the situation. He spoke with an "aw shucks" grin in his voice. "Gosh, Bear, I don't know what happened really. I don't know if I was pushed or tripped or what, but the next thing I knew I was on my face. I kinda hurt myself too." At this he reached down and patted his knee and then went on. "But I think I'll be OK. That's all I know, Bear," he said with innocent eyes.

Bear looked at him for a minute, then said, "OK, boys, let's get to work. You know what has to be done. Supper is coming directly. We're going to have to work most of the night, and then I'll let some of you go get some rest. The others will have to stay with me as we tech the car with NASCAR in case we got something they don't like, which is probably a lot." There was general laughter from the team at this comment. NASCAR always found something they didn't like. "Tyrone, I'd like to see you for a moment," Bear said as he motioned Tyrone over to him.

He walked over to the corner and Tyrone followed him. Bear spoke in low tones so no one else could hear the conversation.

"Tyrone, I'm letting you go. You're done with the team. I'll give you some cash now and an airline ticket back to Charlotte. We'll have your check in the morning for you, or I can mail it to you in Charlotte—whatever you prefer. I would appreciate it if you would turn in your uniforms as soon as you can and clean out your stuff. I'll call Billy back at the main shop and you can drop by there and finish up."

Tyrone stood silently for a minute as the color flushed up his face and he balled his fists at his side. He sputtered for a minute, incredulous, and then exploded in wrath.

"What! You can't fire me, you, you . . ." For the moment words escaped him. Then he went on, "This here is Orly's team."

Bear interrupted him. "You know better'n that, Tyrone. You know that what I say is the same as Orly saying it."

Then, like the air rushing out of a balloon, Tyrone sort of collapsed and fell in on himself. He unballed his fists and gently slapped his thighs with his open hands. His countenance fell and he looked at Bear. "How come you're doing this to me, Bear?"

"Tyrone, I'm not doing this to you. You've done it to yourself. You got a problem and it affects the team, and we just can't have it upsetting everyone. I'm sorry, but this is the way it has to be."

Tyrone refused to let it go. "What kind of problem do you think I have, Bear? Bear, please don't fire me! Please, Bear."

It would have been easier for Bear if Tyrone would have gotten angry and taken a poke at him. This sudden descent into begging was not only unnerving, it was unexpected and seemed very much out of character.

"Tyrone, I'm going to lay it out for you, OK? You're a racist and a bigot. Your attitude is getting worse and worse. God in his wisdom has put all kinds of people on this earth, some of 'em white and black and yellow and red and all shades in between. Didn't any of us choose what color we were going to be before we were born. God didn't give us that kind of choice. Not only did God put us on this earth, but he put us here to get along with one another. Now I don't know much about anything but racin', and I know a lot about that just like you do. But I do know that disliking somebody, hating them even, like you seem to do, is not good and is plain and simple wrong. Now you know me and Orly are Christians and we take care not to rub anybody's nose in our faith, but I'm going to tell you one thing: When Jesus hung up there on that cross, he did it for all people, no matter what race or color they are. The ground at the foot of that cross is level, and there ain't no one any better'n anyone else. You got a problem, Tyrone, and me an' Orly been hopin' you would somehow straighten out. You are one of the best jackmen in the business and a good mechanic to boot, and you have been a great help to us, and probably even helped us win some races. But to be honest, lately you have been running your mouth, and it is hurting the team."

Bear took a breath and pulled the ever-present shop towel from his back pocket and wiped his hands. "Now that's the way it is, Tyrone. If you can get on with another team, why more power to you. I'll be glad to give a recommendation as to your ability with a jack and your qualifications as a mechanic. You can drive the show-car pickup over to the compound and pick up your stuff in the motor home. Now excuse me, I got work to get done." With that, Bear reached into his pocket and handed Tyrone a white envelope with some cash and a plane ticket in it. Then he turned and walked away.

Tyrone stood speechless with his hand outstretched, clutching the envelope. Then gradually his shoulders

wanted the crew to know, he would tell them. He was the boss, and it was best to leave things alone. In the meantime, Paolo prayed that Doug would show up soon.

Finally Doug came ambling into the garage and motioned for Paolo to come over. He said quietly, "I stashed him at Pastor John and Martha's place. Martha said she would feed him and give him a place to sleep. I told her we would come and get him as soon as we could. Boy, Paolo, he's a scrawny little guy, and he was pretty dirty. I think he was plenty hungry too, but Martha will "mom" him pretty good. You know she will."

Paolo responded, "Man, thanks a lot, Doug. I didn't know what to do with him. He looked so pathetic hanging on that fence. I'm not sure what we're going to do with him now either, but we'll see how it works out. Somehow, I feel the Lord has his hand in the middle of this thing. When I get a chance I'm going to give Alicia a call. Maybe she can tell me what to do with him. At least she speaks Spanish. He's pretty shy, and even if we found someone who spoke Spanish I'm not sure he would open up."

Bear walked up. "What are you two doing? Plotting to take over the world no doubt, and probably at the very least planning on causing me some major grief." Bear said all of this good-naturedly and then went on. "Doug, I need you to run some numbers for me. I want to check some of our settings. Paolo, go up into the hauler and get me the number seven transmission and gear set." Bear was wiping his hands on a red shop rag as he said all this, and then concluded his orders with a nondirected whistle through his teeth and a comment made to no one in particular. "Oh, I love racin'! It's so much fun for a tired, puny, old man like me to havta work all night on an ignorant piece of iron just so the driver can go out and break it again. Yes, indeedy, I love racin'. I truly do."

Just about that time, the driver in question came walking into the garage. He looked pretty spiffy, and from a distance one couldn't tell he had smacked the wall, gotten burned, and been a hero. Bear's demeanor quickly changed when he spotted Orly. Suddenly the look on his face was serious.

"Orly Mann, come over here and talk to me. I got to tell you something that pains me very much," Bear said.

Orly paused to look over the race car with a critical eye and gave Bear a wave over his shoulder. He finished his inspection and walked over to Bear. "You know, Bear, I'm getting scared. I'm starting to like these sponsor functions. I really am beginning to appreciate greasy fried chicken and runny apple pie with lime jello on the side." Orly was in big demand as were all Winston Cup drivers. Sponsors wanted exposure for their bucks, and one way to get it was to show off their drivers to the local folks who worked for the companies. Wherever the circuit raced, Orly was expected to attend some sort of function that gave people a chance to ogle the sponsor's driver. Tonight he probably signed three hundred autographs, and his photographic image would grace a hundred more scrapbooks as he stood with his arm around total strangers. They might be strangers to him, but he was certainly not to them. Orly was a popular figure, and it was one aspect of the sport he didn't like much. He was a private man, yet could hardly go out in public anymore without being asked for an autograph or accosted in some way. He was good natured about it though. After all, it was the fans who bought the products the sponsors made and paid the outrageous price for the tickets to the race. It was also the fans who bought the T-shirts and hats and all the other stuff that showed their allegiance to their favorite driver.

Orly walked over to Bear. "Whatta you want, Bear, my man?"

"Orly, I have to make a confession and I don't like it much either, but I was the one that got you hurt this afternoon. It was me that left the track bar loose, and I can't tell you how embarrassed I am about it. I got started and then somebody interrupted me, and the next thing I know I let you go out with the thing loose. I'm sorry, Orly." Bear spoke in a rush with a sheepish look on his face.

"Did you tell the boys?" asked Orly.

"Course I did, Orly. You know I would."

"Yeah, I know you would. Hey, Bear, it doesn't matter now. It's over. It's not like I never made a mistake and wrecked a car. This is racin', as you say, Bear. It was just one of them 'racin' deals.' I know it won't happen again."

"Yeah, it won't happen again, but I'm sorry."

"Hey, it's a done deal. Let's forget it." Orly changed the subject. "How bad we hurt here? Anything left worth saving or are we going to the backup?"

For the next few minutes, the conversation went high tech as Bear and Orly discussed the damage and what Bear had in mind for fixing the car. Then the conversation moved to the best way to set up the car for Sunday's race. It was nearly midnight when Orly took off and headed back to the motor home compound.

The work went on nonstop all night. The race car came apart like a peeled onion until it was essentially a bunch of unconnected pieces laying around the garage. Each piece had its own little congregation as the men worked to bring order to the bent and broken parts.

Bear sent Paolo, Doug, and two other crewmen back to the motor home around one in the morning to get some sleep. He told them to be back by six to relieve the guys who worked all night. By the time Paolo and Doug got back to the garage, the car was going back together like an overgrown puzzle, looking once again like a race car. Two hours later it was loaded back in the hauler, and except for some of the sponsor decals and still damp paint, was pretty much together. It would still need a ton of tweakin', as Bear would say, but now they had some time to fine-tune it.

The crew was sitting down munching donuts and drinking the ever-present strong coffee nicknamed "sludge." Paolo was tired and dirty. Even though he didn't much care for coffee, he was trying to gag some of it down. He glanced over to see Bear and Bud both looking at him. He turned to look over his shoulder to see if maybe they were looking at something or someone behind him. Nope, it was him they were looking at. He looked back sheepishly. Finally Bear pointed a blunt dirty finger at him and beckoned him to come over. Paolo got up and walked over to the two men.

"I'll keep it short, Paolo," said Bear. "I fired Tyrone last night and now we need someone to be the jackman. I want you to take the job. You know that Bud here is the pit-crew boss. He directs the Thunderfoot Ballet Company and his word goes. Now both me and Bud think you can handle this position, so whatta you say?"

"You mean you want me to handle the jack on all the pit stops? Are you sure, Bear? I don't think I even know how to do it. When I did it yesterday, I just did it because somebody needed to. You and Bud were trying to get under the car and Tyrone was down. Golly, Bear, are you sure?"

Bear smiled at Bud. "See, I told you. Yup, we want you to do it and right now you don't have any bad habits. Bud is going to teach you everything you need to know, and you'll do just fine. If you would have bragged to us that you could do it easy, we both would have had second thoughts. But the one good thing—well, actually there are many—but maybe the most important thing about you, Paolo, is that you're teachable. So when Bud teaches you, pay attention. There—it's a done deal." With that, Bear stuck out his hand and Paolo shook it. Bud did the same.

Paolo smiled big this time and turned around to see that the whole crew was looking at him. Most of the guys were smiling with him. They knew that the jackman had to be quick and precise. In a four-tire green-flag pit stop, he had to fly over the wall and race to the right side of the car cradling the special, lightweight jack. One quick pump and the car was in the air high enough to change the tires. Then as soon as the new tires were slammed on the hubs, he had to twist the handle and drop the jack. Then it was a race back to the left side of the car to repeat the process, being careful not to tangle feet with the front-tire changer or get caught in the air hose. In the meantime, the competitors would be squealing into the pit stalls with locked brakes on both sides of them, adding danger and confusion to the whole procedure. It could be scary and it could also be very dangerous. Paolo's moves dictated the overall speed of the pit stop. A quick stop meant a faster race, and many a race had been won in the pits by a good crew. Track position could be gained or lost by the speed of the crew. The Thunderfoot Ballet Company was the best, and Paolo would have to work hard to maintain the level of excellence. He would have to be a capable student and a fast learner. A couple of the crewmen looked at him carefully with sullen looks of calculation. Despite his shortcomings, Tyrone was an excellent jackman and knew his business. They were a bit more cautious. Time would tell.

Paolo finally got a break and slipped out of the garage to call Alicia. He could have used the team cell phone, but he wanted to talk to her privately. The phone rang and a heavily accented Chinese voice answered, "Hello."

"Hello Aunty Grandmother, this is Paolo." Paolo chuckled to himself. He wondered which Aunty Grandmother he was speaking to. He went on, "I wonder if I might speak to Alicia, please."

The voice on the other end of the line smiled and said, "Oh yeah, Pally. I get her for you."

A minute later Alicia's soft voice answered, "Hi Pally. I'm so glad you called. I have been worrying about you. Are you OK?"

"Hi Alicia. Yeah, I'm OK. Howzit going there?" asked Paolo.

"Well, it's interesting to say the least. Something is going on here, but they won't tell me. They just keep looking at me with . . . oh, I don't know how to describe it . . . anyway, things are a little weird here. Hey Pally, what is going on there? I saw Orly's crash on the news and the fire and everything. Is he alright really? And who was that guy poking you in the chest? Boy, Pally, I thought you were going to punch him. Did you know the camera got a real close-up of you two? Gracious, what was going on?"

Paolo let her run down a little then interrupted with, "I'll tell you later. Alicia, listen to me. I need your help. I have a situation here. Do you remember Juan-Jesus from Mexicali?"

"Juan-Jesus? Sure I do, Pally. A little guy. He lives with his mom and two sisters on the other side of the canal over by Ramona's lot. Why do you ask? What's going on?"

"Alicia, is there any chance the grandmothers would let you use their car to take a run over here? There is so much going on right now and I really need to talk to you. Juan-Jesus is here in Daytona at the racetrack! I don't have any idea why he's here or what he's doing, but I think he needs to talk to somebody he knows and trusts. Right now he's at Pastor John's motor home. You remember him from Sears Point." Paolo paused, then went on, "Do you think you could?"

"Yes, of course, I remember Pastor John and Martha. I stayed in their motor home that one night." Alicia knew Paolo very well and could hear the worry and anxiety in his voice.

"Hang on, Paolo, let me check." Alicia laid the phone down and went to talk with the Aunty Grandmothers. Paolo could hear the faint conversation in Chinese. It seemed to go on forever, but finally Alicia came back.

"Yes, I can make it work, Pally. What time and where should I meet you?"

"That's great! I'm sorry, but it will have to be this evening after the garage closes for the night. We've been working on the car all night, and we have to run the thing through tech this morning so Orly can practice this afternoon. Then Bud and the Ballet Company want to sit down with me and go over some stuff."

Alicia noticed that Paolo was using the racin' language just like Bear. In fact, when he talked about the car, he was using the same slang terms Bear used. Paolo went on, "Man, it is getting wild here, Alicia. Bear fired Tyrone— that's the guy who had his finger in my face—and now they've made me the jackman of the Ballet Company. Maybe you'll see me during the race or somethin'. At any rate, I gotta practice pit stops with the team. Bud, you know, Doug's dad, is working with me, and I gotta learn everything all at once. Pray for me Alicia, will you? I'm pretty nervous about this whole thing, but Bear thinks I can . . . listen to me ramble on. Here's what we'll do. Me and Doug and Juan-Jesus will meet you in the Target store parking lot at six o'clock tonight. How's that?"

"That's good, Pally. I'll have to watch myself because if I get home too late, they'll worry. I'll see you guys then. Tell Juan-Jesus that Alicia says *hola.*"

"Thanks, Alicia." Paolo finished the conversation and hung up the phone. By the time he walked back into the shop, Jimmy had the hauler backed up to the door again and they were loading the race car. *I wonder how Juan-Jesus is doing,* thought Paolo.

As a matter of fact Juan-Jesus was just now sitting up in the bunk and rubbing the sleep out of his eyes, and he was doing pretty good. He'd slept for nearly fourteen hours, and as he stretched he noticed that his jeans and T-shirt were folded at the foot of the bed. They had been washed and, though threadbare, were at least clean. He climbed out of the bed and hit the bathroom. When he came out, he was dressed with his face washed and his hair slicked back. Martha was busy at the stove and looked up to see him coming. She smiled at him and said, *"Buenos dias Señor. Comer, por favor."*

Juan-Jesus was far too polite to correct her rough Spanish. The smell emanating from the stove made him take a seat in the dining alcove. He smiled back at Martha as she spooned the sausage and scrambled eggs on his plate. He bowed his head and said a quick prayer of thanks and dove in.

Just as Juan-Jesus was finishing up, Pastor John opened the door to the motor home and entered with another man on his heels. The other man was young and dressed in a team uniform and obviously connected to a stock car team.

"Martha, you know Tony. I brought him over to see if he could talk with this young man, and maybe we could figure out how best to help him."

Tony slid into the booth opposite Juan-Jesus and smiled at him. Juan-Jesus looked back at him but continued to eat. Tony spoke in perfect Spanish.

"Hey, kid, how ya doing? Looks like Mrs. Martha is feeding you pretty good. They're wondering where you're from and what you're doing here. By the way, what's your name?"

Juan-Jesus looked up from his plate and said in a soft voice, "My name is Juan-Jesus Lopez Mendoza, and I am a locksmith."

Tony waited for him to go on, but Juan-Jesus said no more.

"I see, Mr. Mendoza. You are a locksmith. Might I ask what you are doing at the Daytona International Speedway? From the look of you, the locksmithing business hasn't been so good lately."

Juan-Jesus finished his plate and kept his eyes downcast. He said nothing for a while, then spoke softly again. "I'm not sure where this place is, but I must get to Florida. I have something very important that I must do, and I must do it very soon."

Tony smiled and spoke to Pastor John and Martha in English. "He says his name is Juan-Jesus Lopez Mendoza and that he is a locksmith and must get to Florida to do something very important. So far, that's all he'll tell me." Tony turned to Juan-Jesus again.

"Look, kid, you are in Florida. Now tell us where you are from and where your parents are. Are you running from something? Have you done something wrong? If you don't tell us what is going on, we will have to call the police, and they will probably turn you over to Immigration unless you are a citizen. Are you the one who hid in Orly's show-car trailer?

Juan-Jesus replied, "Yes, I hid in the trailer and no, I'm not from here." Then he went silent and kept his head down.

Tony asked him repeated questions, but Juan-Jesus refused to answer. The more Tony pressed him, the lower he sunk in the seat. Finally, the tears started leaking from his eyes. Martha spoke.

"OK Tony, that's enough. He isn't ready to talk yet. He looks pretty upset. Just ask him if he has a friend here."

Tony asked Juan-Jesus the question and waited patiently for his reply.

Finally Juan-Jesus spoke, and Tony turned to Pastor John and Martha.

"Yeah, he says he has two friends here. One is Jesus. I think he means the Lord Jesus. And the second is a guy named Paolo or Palito. That's all he will say." Tony slid out of the alcove.

"I'm sorry, guys, but he doesn't want to talk much. He seems to be real afraid, so I don't know what to tell you. I gotta get back to the garage. If you need me, John, you know where to find me." With that, he was out the door and gone.

Pastor John and Martha stood next to the stove and pondered the young Mexican boy sitting in the booth with downcast eyes.

Tyrone stared at the institutional green paint peeling off the wall of the Daytona Beach city jail and considered his miserable circumstances. His head hurt, he had a bad taste in his mouth, and he was hungover. His memory of the night before was foggy, but he knew for certain that he had wrecked Orly's show-car pickup. After leaving the garage, he had stopped at a liquor store and picked up a six-pack of beer and, on a whim, a bottle of cheap whiskey to go with it. He drove down to the beach, parked, and then proceeded to drink himself into oblivion. After that the details started to get fuzzy, but he vaguely remembered bouncing the truck off an innocent palm tree. Then the world erupted in whirling red lights and handcuffs and here he was. He was not a drinker by nature, but he did appreciate a cold beer now and then. He seldom if ever drank anything stronger, but the whiskey seemed like a good way to escape his problems for a while. It didn't work very well, because now he had more problems and a hangover to go with them. Man, he felt bad.

The deputy clanged down the corridor through the gates and put a key in the door of Tyrone's cell. "Alright, Wallace, you've been bailed out. Come on, let's go. I hate to tell you this, pal, but you don't smell so good. You don't look so good neither. Come on, your ride is waiting."

Tyrone carefully raised himself up off the concrete bunk and followed the deputy out the door. His befuddled brain was trying to sort out who might have bailed him out. Didn't seem like he had many friends left anymore. He stopped at the booking desk to sign out for his valuables and turned to face Orly Mann.

"I'm sorry, Orly. I don't know what to say. I feel fairly foolish and a whole bunch stupid."

Orly looked at Tyrone with a lopsided grin. "Well, Hoss, I would say that what you're feeling is probably pretty right on. Come get your stuff. You can clean up at my place. I gotta get moving—we've got a practice in about an hour."

🏁🏁

Back at Pastor John and Martha's motor home, Juan-Jesus finally raised his head and unfolded his arms. He slid out of the alcove and said to Martha in Spanish, "Thank you very much for allowing me to sleep in your house and eat your food. Thank you also for washing my clothes. Your hospitality has been very gracious, but I must go now."

Martha caught only part of what he said, but she nodded her head and started to pat his shoulder, then thought better of it. Her intuition told her that Juan-Jesus was trying very hard to be a man so she would treat him like one.

With that, Juan-Jesus went out the door of the motor home and down the steps. He looked around, surveying the area, and made a conscious decision to sit down on the ground and wait. Three hours later, Martha brought him a Coke and a plate full of sandwiches surrounded by potato chips. Juan-Jesus smiled at her and said, *"Muchas gracias"* and proceeded to eat everything, including the crumbs.

Pastor John watched Juan-Jesus out the window and wondered where the kid stored all that food. He didn't look big enough to hold that much.

🏁

Paolo was tired, but it was a good tired. The whole crew was tired and even Bear was starting to slow down a little. The car was back together and had been ushered through the tech procedure. For once, NASCAR was happy. All the templates fit and the other inspections were within the parameters of the rules. Bear watched the procedure like the proverbial hawk. He didn't mind rules, but they better be the same for everybody and he was going to use them to whatever advantage he could, which was a typical mind-set for a crew chief. The safety stuff was dead on. Bear never took chances with the important stuff. It was one reason he felt so bad about yesterday.

An hour later, Orly took the car out for a shakedown in the afternoon practice session, and he immediately liked what he felt. His experience and general capability told him that the car was right. It was not only "right"—it was "good," which in racing parlance meant that it had potential. After four laps he brought it back in and the fine-tuning process began. For the next hour and a half, Orly would run a few laps, and then the crew would change shocks and springs and make adjustments to the track bar and other suspension components. Each time Orly went out, Doug reported lower lap times over the radio. By the end of the session, even Bear was smiling, and the other teams were noting the fact that Orly was beginning to match times with the fastest group of cars. Finally the session ended and the crew packed it up for the day. Everybody was tired, but it had been a pretty good day. At least they had managed to put something decent under Orly.

As soon as they could get away, Paolo and Doug headed over to Pastor John and Martha's motor home. They came loping through the gate with long strides, and Juan-Jesus spotted them fifty yards away. He stood up, brushed the dirt off the seat of his pants, and smiled a broad, toothy grin as Paolo came walking up. Suddenly the man part disappeared, and the little Mexican kid from the barrio came to the surface as Juan-Jesus threw himself into Paolo's arms and buried his head on his chest. Paolo hugged him for a moment, then looked at Doug, "It's OK.

133

"We're going to meet Alicia—you remember her from Sears Point last year? We're going to meet her in a few minutes. She speaks good Spanish and she knows him like me. He might open up to her." As Paolo spoke he ruffled Juan-Jesus's hair. "Thanks, you guys, for keeping an eye on him. We'll let you know how things work out."

"No problem, Paolo. Glad to help out. He's a very nice young man and we appreciated having him around," said Martha.

With that, the good-byes were said and the two young men walked back to the garage area accompanied by one small Mexican boy who felt safer than he had in days walking between them.

Now maybe he could get on with his mission . . .

Starting a quarrel is like breaching a dam; so drop the matter before a dispute breaks out.

Proverbs 17:14

"I enjoyed it. The good days were great, but the bad days were twice as bad. There were good days and bad days."

Gary DeHart, retired crew chief

ALICIA WAS FIGHTING the Friday night race traffic, and she was late. It wasn't unusual for her to be late. Paolo often said he had yet to see her be on time for anything. That was unfair, she thought. She was on time for a lot of things; she just didn't have a good sense of time. Having just gotten her driver's license in San Francisco a few months ago, she was not a very experienced driver. She was driving the Aunty Grandmothers' ancient Cadillac and having a tough time adjusting to its size. She was almost lost in the big overstuffed seats and felt like she was sitting in a recliner in the living room. In fact driving this thing was a lot like driving the living room. Maybe the whole house.

Alicia finally crept to Speedway Boulevard and eased her way through the stoplights until she spotted the Target store. The parking lot was jam-packed with race-weekend shoppers, and she swiveled her neck looking for Paolo as she herded the Caddy up and down the rows of cars. How like Paolo to just assume she would know what kind of car they would be driving. Just when she was about to give up, she saw a young Hispanic boy looking out the window of a parked car as she crept past. He couldn't see her through the tinted windows of the Cadillac, but she could see him and recognized Juan-Jesus. He had grown some but not much. He seemed to be in the car by himself. Where were Paolo and Doug? Then she looked a little closer and realized that they had both reclined their seats and were sound asleep. That's right, Paolo said they pulled an all-nighter fixing the race car, and both he and Doug were pretty used up. She finally found an empty spot in a back section of the lot, parked the Caddy, grabbed her purse, and walked back to the car.

Juan-Jesus was fiddling with the radio, trying to tune in the distant Spanish radio station while Paolo and Doug dozed in the seats. Finally he got it to come in and smiled as he listened to the announcer tout the latest *bandas* in rapid-fire Spanish. Alicia walked up and rapped on the window. Juan-Jesus turned and his face lit up in a wonderful smile. He threw open the door of the car and flung himself into her arms, muttering, *"Gracias a Dios, gracias a Dios,"* over and over.

She hugged him back and spoke to him in Spanish. "Juan-Jesus, what are you doing here? I'm glad to see you too, but this is amazing. Have you come all the way from Mexicali? Where are you going, and what are you doing? . . ."

Juan-Jesus interrupted her and spoke in machine-gun Spanish, "Alicia, God heard my prayers and brought you here. Palito kept saying your name, but I didn't understand that you would come. I knew we were waiting for somebody. Now I have Paolo and the other man to protect me and you to speak for me. I have a very important thing to do that God has called me to do, and I must do it, and I must do it soon. But I have to get my backpack because it has what I need to find out where I must go." Juan-Jesus continued to speak rapidly as Alicia listened intently.

Both Paolo and Doug woke up looking a little bleary-eyed but happy to see Alicia. She gave them both a wave as she continued to talk to Juan-Jesus.

It always amazed Paolo to hear Alicia speak another language so fluently. It seemed odd that this distinctively Chinese girl, who was now a very beautiful young woman, could communicate so clearly with this young Mexican kid. They had been with Juan-Jesus for hours and were able to communicate only in gestures and single words. Now all of a sudden the barriers were down and Juan-Jesus and Alicia could communicate freely. Paolo turned to Doug. "See, I told you he would open up to her. She has a way about her that makes it easy to talk to her, no matter who you are."

Doug replied, "Yeah, I can see that. You are a very fortunate and blessed guy, Paolo. If she didn't like you so much, I would make a play for her myself. Man, that kid is talking like a faucet that got turned on full blast. I never heard anybody talk that fast."

Paolo pondered that remark and said nothing. Alicia finally turned her attention to Paolo and Doug. "Well, I'm not sure I understand all of it, but he has come from his home in Mexicali. He did hide in the trailer, and I guess the guy driving it—what's his name . . ."

Both Doug and Paolo said at the same time, "Tyrone."

"Tyrone scared him pretty bad and it was a wild trip, but he finally got here. He has something very important to do, but he can't tell me until he gets his backpack, which he says he left in the trailer. He's also very grateful to you guys for taking care of him, and he feels very important that you are protecting him. He says he's very happy and knows that God is going to answer his prayers like always. He also says that you guys should learn Spanish so that you could talk to him."

Doug and Paolo looked at each other. "I wonder if he has thought about learning some English?" asked Doug.

"So what you are saying to us, Alicia, is that we have to find his backpack somewhere. Right? Or at least that's what he wants us to do." said Paolo.

"Yes, Pally, he seems pretty adamant about it. I don't know what else to tell you," said Alicia.

"Why can't he just tell us what is going on?" asked Doug.

"I don't know, Doug, but he says he needs the backpack and until he gets it there isn't anything else to tell."

All three of them stared at Juan-Jesus, and he looked back at them with a smile and raised both his hands with the palms up in the universal gesture that could mean so many different things but mostly . . . that's it—that's all I can say.

139

Tyrone sat in Orly's motor home looking at Orly across the table. He was clean but still feeling fairly miserable. He had tried to nap in the afternoon but it hadn't worked. He contemplated Orly through bloodshot eyes. Orly simply looked back at him.

Finally Tyrone spoke. "So, how's the car?"

"Tyrone, I don't want to talk about the car with you. I've watched you these past months, and you're gradually losing it. Won't be long before you go augering into the dirt like an airplane in a nosedive. What's going on? You never used to be like this. Now you're so full of hate and meanness that nobody wants to be around you."

"Yeah, I know, Orly. I've been a real screwup." Tyrone looked down at his hands on the table.

"I've got to get going. I'm supposed to be interviewed on a radio show in a few minutes. Stay here as long as you like. Don't do anything else stupid. You owe me the bail money, and I want you to cover whatever the insurance doesn't on the truck. Oh yeah, I would stay out of Bear's way. He isn't too happy with you right now."

"Am I still fired, Orly?"

"Yes, indeed, you're still fired, Tyrone." With that, Orly was up and out the door.

After a few minutes, Tyrone got up and went out the door himself. He walked through the motor home compound with his hands in his pockets and then, almost as if his steps were guided, he found himself in front of Pastor John and Martha's place. He knocked on the door.

John opened the door and said, "Hello, Tyrone. Orly said you might be dropping by. Come on in. Martha isn't here. She's over at a shower for one of the wives."

Tyrone came in and sat down while John fixed coffee. Nothing was said for a few minutes, and then Tyrone began to speak in a low voice, with his head down.

"It ain't been easy, John, since he died. He was only seven, you know, and it was like I couldn't do anything to help him. The disease just ate him up, and no matter what chemo they tried or whatever they did it just didn't help. He just got sicker. I used to sit beside him and pray that God would give me the disease for a while so he could be a time without hurtin'. Then when he passed, it was like I lost a part of me, like a hand or something. I couldn't do anything for a while. Me and Janey did OK, and then it came down on both of us real hard that he was gone and wasn't ever gonna come back. That's when we started takin' it out on each other, I guess. Then pretty soon she got tired of me and was gone. Went back home to live with her mom. Now she's filed for divorce. Got the papers two months ago." Tyrone looked up at John, then went on, "Pretty sad story, huh? Now I lost my job and I wrecked the company truck, and I'll probably go to jail." Tyrone put his face in his hands and wept. He groaned in a muffled voice, "I miss my boy so much. I couldn't do nothin', John. I couldn't do nothin' to help him." His broad shoulders heaved with his sobs.

John kept his mouth shut and simply listened. Tyrone went on pouring out his anguish. It was obvious to John that Tyrone had been saving this up for a long time, and now it was like opening up a septic wound. Bitterness and pain came gushing out. John patiently waited for the hurt to subside. After a while Tyrone stopped sobbing.

Tyrone looked at John and asked the question the pastor had been praying he might ask.

"John, what do I do? I can't go on like this. When I look down the road, I don't see nothin' but blackness. I just can't go on like this much longer."

John responded, "Well, there is a way, and there is one who gives guidance because he knows what it is to hurt and to be in pain. His name is Jesus, Tyrone. No doubt you have heard about him, but I don't think you know him." John then went on to tell Tyrone about Jesus and compassion. About his gentleness and kindness and sweet spirit. He told Tyrone about Jesus' sacrifice and willingness to stay beside us in even the darkest circumstances. Most of all, John told Tyrone about Jesus' love.

Tyrone had many questions that John couldn't answer. He freely admitted that he didn't understand all the whys and wherefores either, but he did understand that Jesus was faithful through it all.

The discussion went on for two hours and through two pots of coffee. Then there was a knock at the door, and John opened it to let Orly in. Orly slid into the alcove and looked at Tyrone.

"How ya doing, Hoss?"

"I'm doing better, Orly. I'm glad you came. I always wanted to ask you this, but I guess I never figured it was any of my business. Maybe I shouldn't ask it now." Tyrone looked down.

"It's all right, Tyrone. I think I know what you want to ask me. Go ahead."

"How did you do it, Orly, when you lost your wife and daughter?"

"I didn't do it, Tyrone. I was just as crazy as you, and I have to admit I had a lot of questions for God. It was like my heart got ripped right out of my chest, and I just didn't think I could live anymore. We had just won the championship and things were looking real rosy. As a matter of fact, they couldn't have been better. Then God, for reasons only he understands, took them home to be with him. It took me a long time to come to grips with it, and in truth I haven't done that fully; but I rest in his strength and power and let him carry me through day by day and minute by minute. One thing that helped a bunch was doing my best to keep from focusing on myself all the time. Ask John. He knows all about it. I practically lived with him and Martha for a while." Orly said all this with a look of compassion on his face. He truly did understand Tyrone's pain.

"The whole deal begins with putting your faith in Jesus, Tyrone. That's where it starts."

🏁

Doug, Paolo, Alicia, and Juan-Jesus sat in the car with the lights off and contemplated the police impound lot. They could see the show-car pickup through the fence. They could also see the sign that said two things. The first was in big letters and said simply, "NO TRESPASSING. POLICE IMPOUND AREA." Then in small letters it said, "All Police Business Must Be Taken Care of Between the Hours of 9 A.M. and 5 P.M."

Juan-Jesus said to Alicia, "That looks like the pretty truck that pulled the trailer I rode in from California."

"It is," she said, "and we think it's where your backpack and jacket are. But we can't get in to get it until tomorrow."

"Why not?" Juan-Jesus asked.

"Because the gate is locked and there's no way to get in. We certainly can't climb the fence." She was joking but Juan-Jesus didn't realize it.

Then, before anyone realized what was happening, Juan-Jesus was out of the car and running to the gate. It was secured with a large padlock and a chain. He reached into his back pocket and brought out the little leather case with the assorted tools and blanks. In just a few minutes, the lock popped open, to the amazement of Alicia, Paolo, and Doug.

Doug whispered, "Man, he did that quick. This kid knows what he's doing."

Alicia said, "Guys, I don't like this. This is the police lot and we're trespassing. I'm not sure we should go in." While Alicia was speaking, Juan-Jesus had already opened the gate and was just about to make a run for the pickup.

Paolo hissed, "Juan-Jesus, wait a minute!" But it was too late. Thirty seconds later the whole lot lit up like daylight and a voice boomed over hidden loudspeakers with the command, "This is the police! Remain where you are and raise your hands over your heads. I repeat: This is the police!"

Bear had just laid his head down on the pillow when the cellular phone rang next to his ear. Bud Prescott reached over from the other bunk and picked it up.

"Hey, Doug, what's up? How come you guys aren't in bed?" Suddenly Bud sat up and swung his legs over the edge of the bunk. "You're where? What in the Sam Hill are you doing there? You're with who? Alicia too? Doug, you better have a good explanation for this. Yeah, I'll be down there in a few minutes. Where's the place again?" He turned the phone off and looked over at Bear.

"You're not gonna believe this . . . they're in jail."

Bear opened his eyes and stifled a yawn in midstream. "Jail! Who? Doug? What'd he do?"

"Not just Doug but Paolo, Alicia, and that Hispanic kid too."

"Did you find out where the place is?" asked Bear as he reached for his pants.

A half hour later, Bear and Bud were standing in front of the sergeant's desk, explaining that, yes, they did know these young people and, yes, the orange pickup that was wrecked did belong to the Orly Mann Racing Team and, yes, the kids were just trying to retrieve something out of it. No, no one would say how the gate got opened.

The desk sergeant looked at Bear and Bud. "Lemme see now if I got this right. This big kid with the curly hair works for you," he said, pointing at Bear. Then he went on, "Now this tall kid is your son," he said, pointing at Bud. Bud nodded. "And lemme see, this young lady is a friend and she's staying in Orlando. I better call her folks there." Alicia suddenly felt faint. She could just imagine what mayhem would occur if all of the three Aunty Grandmothers got the word that she was being detained at the police station. If he called them, he better call the paramedics first.

The desk sergeant went on. "Now who does this guy belong to?" he asked, pointing at Juan-Jesus.

Paolo interrupted, "Oh, he's my cousin. He's Bear's sister's boy, David. Right, David?" said Paolo, nodding at Juan-Jesus.

Juan-Jesus looked at the desk sergeant and said one of the fourteen words he knew in English, "Yes."

The desk sergeant looked the group over carefully and then said, "Is that right, Bear?"

Bear's eyebrows disappeared into his hairline and then he replied, "Well, I come from a big family."

The desk sergeant made up his mind. "Well, I guess you guys can go. You're still not sure how that gate got opened, huh?" He looked straight at Juan-Jesus. Juan-Jesus looked back and saw the imperceptible shake of the head from Paolo.

"No," Juan-Jesus replied.

The desk sergeant dismissed them with a wave of his hand and then spoke to Bear. "Hey, Bear, how's it looking for Orly and you guys on Sunday? I was out at the track this afternoon, and Orly was clicking off some pretty good lap times." The ensuing conversation focused around the race on Sunday as Bear and Bud schmoozed with the guy for a few minutes. Bud made a signal behind his back, and the young people made a beeline for the exit. Paolo had a strong grip on Juan-Jesus's shoulder.

They stood on the curb in front of the police station and looked at each other. Finally, Doug couldn't stand it any longer and broke into laughter. It was catching and as the tension faded, everybody was giggling. The laughter suddenly stopped when Bear and Bud appeared.

Bear took charge and looked the group over with a frown. "All right, who's going to go first and tell me and Bud what's going on? By the way, hi Alicia, it's nice to see you again. Seems like every time I see you, it's late at night and has something to do with a fence of some sort. And who is this who happens to be the nephew of my third cousin of my sister, of which I have none, Mr. Paolo man?" said Bear, gesturing to Juan-Jesus.

Then everyone tried to talk at once, including Juan-Jesus. Bear threw his hands up and said to Bud, "I think we need to go over to Perkins and sort this out over some pie and coffee. Whatta you think?"

"Makes sense to me, and it's the only thing that does so far," replied Bud.

A while later, the group was ensconced in a corner booth and feeling much better after pie and ice cream. Once again Juan-Jesus outdid himself to the quiet amazement of everyone as he devoured an enormous piece of peach pie and a large scoop of ice cream.

"So let me see if I got this right," said Bear. "This is the kid who stowed away in the trailer and came here from California. He's in the country illegally, and that's why I all of a sudden had a nephew. You were afraid the police would find out he didn't have any ID and hold him for Immigration. He lost his backpack and needs it so he can tell us why he's here. You guys went to the trailer at the compound first and looked there, but the backpack wasn't there. So you assumed that it might be in the pickup, which Tyrone wrecked last night and the police impounded. Am I right so far?"

Everyone nodded, and Juan-Jesus looked up from scraping a bit of ice cream off the plate to say, "Yessss," then went back to work.

"So where we stand right now is that we still don't know where the backpack might be? Right?" said Bear. Then he went on, "Well, I know where it is. How's that?

You shoulda asked old Bear right from the git-go and saved everybody a lot of grief."

The group sat in silence, waiting for Bear to elaborate.

"Now, here's what we're gonna do. According to my watch, it's just past eleven. You two boys haven't had any sleep to speak of since yesterday, and I need you sharp for tomorrow. Paolo, we got training in the morning for pit stops, and if you're gonna be the jackman you need all the practice you can get. Alicia, you're already late and were supposed to be in Orlando, which is two hours away, an hour ago. I'm not real comfortable thinking about you driving home this late at night, so why don't you call home and then spend the night with Pastor John and Martha. I'll set that up for you. We'll take Señor Zorro here home with us," Bear said, motioning to Juan-Jesus. "Then come morning, we'll get the backpack and sort the rest of this thing out. Whatta you say to that?"

It seemed like a plan. Alicia agreed that Bear was right. It was too far to try to go home tonight.

There was a pay phone in the lobby of the restaurant so Alicia took the opportunity to call the Aunty Grandmothers. When she called, she had to talk to each one to assure them that she was all right. After ten minutes of explanation, they reluctantly agreed that she should stay.

Alicia and the guys picked up the old Caddy at the Target parking lot on the way back to the track, and Paolo drove it for her.

As Paolo herded the thing down the road, they talked. "Boy, what a night. What do you suppose this is all about Alicia?" he asked.

"I don't know, Pally, he won't tell me yet. He will eventually though. When we get his backpack, I'm sure it will make sense. He's really dead set on accomplishing whatever it is that he needs to do. That much is for sure."

Paolo looked into the rearview mirror and saw Juan-Jesus smiling back at him. He was in the middle of the big backseat with his arms thrown back and looking very much like a movie star relaxing in a limo. He said to Alicia in Spanish, "Tell Palito not to worry. God is in control. I know he'll work everything out. Tell Palito if he continues to frown like that, his eyebrows will grow together like Mr. Bear." Then he laughed.

"What did he say, Alicia?"

"Uh, he said not to worry and that he's sorry for all the grief he's caused you—or something like that," she told him.

"Yeah, right," Paolo grunted.

Martha was delighted to see Alicia again and was glad to put her up for the night. John wasn't home yet. He was making a call, Martha explained. She put the teapot on so Alicia could tell her all about Juan-Jesus, at least what she knew so far anyway. Alicia told Martha about the youth group from the church in San Francisco ministering in Mexicali and how she had seen Juan-Jesus grow up as a kid. It was late when they finally called it a night. Pastor John still had not returned home.

As Alicia got ready for bed, she contemplated the events of the evening. Juan-Jesus was laughing on the outside, but she could tell that he was dealing with something very

149

heavy. He told her that he'd been very scared on this whole trip, but since God had led him to Paolo things were much better. Now that she was here, he was certain that God was going to answer his prayers. It was a matter of life and death, but he wouldn't say whose. Well, she would deal with it as it came tomorrow. With that, she rolled over and went to sleep.

Bear sent the boys with Bud to the motor home. He told them he had to make a quick stop and would be there in a few minutes. When he found his way to Orly's motor home, the light was still on. He knocked gently and then went in. Orly, Tyrone, and John were all sitting around the table.

"I see you boys are keeping my driver up too late this night," said Bear. Then he looked at them a little closer. "I'm sorry for interruptin'. It looks like you guys are involved in something serious, but, Tyrone, it's you I was lookin' for. Do you know where that backpack is that that kid left in the trailer?"

"Yeah, I do, Bear. In fact, I've got it right here. Me and John and Orly here was just discussin' it. We were over at John's, but we didn't wanna keep Martha up so we moved to Orly's. Would ya mind sittin' down for a minute?" asked Tyrone.

The name of the LORD is a strong tower; the righteous run to it and are safe.

Proverbs 18:10

"If we can keep the driver from getting banged up this year, hopefully we can run strong all year."

Larry McReynolds, crew chief, Winston Cup car #31

BEAR BASKED in the early morning sunshine, drinking coffee in a comfortable folding chair next to the motor home. It was Saturday and there was no rush this morning. The Busch Series race would be run this day, and the next Winston Cup practice session wasn't scheduled until later this afternoon. There would be plenty to do then, but in the meantime everyone could slow down just a little and sleep in an extra half hour or so. Bear reminded himself that he had to get the Ballet Company together soon and help Bud integrate Paolo into the program. He'll make a fine jackman, Bear thought. He's strong, agile, and very quick. Quicker than he knows or realizes. He'll be smart enough to do exactly as we say. No more, no less. Yeah, he'll do fine. Bear looked up at the sky and noticed the high, wispy clouds. Weather's going to change some, which will shuffle the deck. Daytona was one of those places where track temperature and cloud cover could really change the handling dynamics of a car. It could also affect fuel mileage and horsepower. Bear would have to be very careful about how he jetted the carburetor.

As Bear drank his coffee, the door to the motor home opened and Juan-Jesus stepped out into the early morning light. He was clutching the worn backpack to his chest with both hands. He looked at Bear for a minute, then came over and sat down in a chair next to him.

"Buenos dias, Señor Bear," said Juan-Jesus

Bear looked at him with a gentle grin. "And the same to you my little friend. I suppose you're hungry now?" Bear made a motion of eating while he spoke.

Juan-Jesus looked at him gravely and then made his own motion of eating while nodding his head. "Yes, I could eat a little something, Mr. Bear," he said in Spanish.

"Well, let's you and me take a little walk over to the hospitality tent and see if we can't scare up something to . . . how do you say it? *Comer* . . . yeah, that's it. Let's you and me go *comer*." With that, he got up, put his arm around Juan-Jesus's shoulders, and the two of them headed for the food area.

Juan-Jesus kept a tight two-handed grip on the backpack as they walked along.

As they approached the food area, they could smell that breakfast was indeed being served. Pastor John, Martha, and Alicia were sitting at a table finishing their breakfast and drinking coffee. As soon as Juan-Jesus saw Alicia, he broke into a run and plopped into a chair beside her.

"Look, Alicia, I have my backpack. I woke up this morning and there it was on my bed next to me. I don't know how it got there, but here it is." Juan-Jesus held out the backpack like a precious treasure for all to see.

"Yes, I see that, Juan-Jesus. Now maybe you will tell us why you needed it so badly, and maybe you can tell us why you're here and what it is you must do," said Alicia in her best Spanish.

"Yes, I will tell you now." Juan-Jesus carefully placed the backpack on the table and unzipped the cover. Pastor John, Martha, Bear, and Alicia all waited expectantly as Juan-Jesus stuck his hand inside and brought out the contents piece by piece. As he pulled each item out, he carefully arranged them in an order that made sense only to him. Once he had everything on the table, he looked it over carefully and smoothed things down with careful hands. Then he began to speak.

"This is a picture of my family. It was taken before my papa died. This is my papa, and this is my mama and my sisters, Maria and Angelica. This is me in the middle." Everyone leaned over the table to see the formal picture of a Mexican family. Papa and Mama were sitting and the children were grouped around them.

"This is a picture of my sister Angelica. She is eight years old and is very sick." Juan-Jesus held up a second picture for everyone to see. Angelica was a beautiful little girl with bright eyes and long black hair. Whoever had taken the picture had managed to catch her shy little smile. Again, everyone around the table leaned forward to see better, and no one said a word. Finally Alicia said, "That is his sister."

Next, Juan-Jesus picked up a manila envelope with the name Angelica Lopez Mendoza written along the top. Below Angelica's name was the name of a doctor. The envelope was thick with what appeared to be medical documents.

"These are the papers that the doctor gave us, and they tell us what is wrong with my sister. The doctor says that she has a bad sickness called leukemia." He pronounced "leukemia" in English.

Bear, Pastor John, and Martha exchanged looks.

Juan-Jesus went on. "The doctor said that she is not getting well with the . . . how do you say it . . . the chemotherapy. He said that maybe if she could get a bone marrow transplant she might get well." He said "chemotherapy" and "bone marrow transplant" in accented English. Juan-Jesus looked intently at the faces around the table. "She must have this thing. I am not sure what this thing is, but she must have it. It is very important." He paused only long enough for Alicia to translate for the others.

Juan-Jesus put the envelope down and picked up another paper. It was a copy of a newspaper article that was heavily smudged and dog-eared. It looked like it had been read many times. "Then I saw this article in our Mexicali newspaper when I was selling papers on the boulevard by the bull ring. It tells how they sometimes take the blood from a brother or sister and they can help the one who is sick. This article tells how they do this in Florida, so I determined that I must go to Florida and get this thing done so I can help Angelica get well again. I could give her my blood and then she would get well. Then maybe my mama won't have to worry so much. She misses my papa and she has to work so hard. I am a man now and I know how to do the locksmithing, but I am not as good as my papa was." As Juan-Jesus said this he blinked back sudden tears.

After scanning the article Alicia turned to the group. "I think we have it figured out. He left Mexicali to come to Florida because he read this article about the National Bone Marrow Donor Program. Maybe you guys know how it works. It says they take blood samples from folks and match the samples with those who have various diseases, leukemia being one of them. After a suitable match is found, then they take bone marrow from the healthy individual and inject it into the bloodstream of the sick person. I guess for some people it really gives them a chance to beat the disease and live a normal life. It doesn't always work, and I guess it isn't for everyone. The big problem is finding the right donors. Sometimes siblings have the best chance of being a good match."

Alicia paused for a moment and then went on. "At any rate, that's why he's here. He was heading to the Donor Program office in Florida. I don't think he really has a concept of where in Florida. It just seemed to him that if he could get to Florida, he would find the right place."

Juan-Jesus picked up the tattered map that lay next to the papers on the table. "Florida, yes. That is where I must go." He unfolded the map and showed everyone the line from California and the circle he had drawn around Florida. "See, it is right here. Is this where I am?" he asked Alicia.

"Yes, Juan-Jesus, you are in Florida. But Florida is a big place. It's a state, you know, like Frontera in Mexico." Alicia put her finger on the map indicating Daytona.

Juan-Jesus showed some irritation and spoke back, "I know that Alicia. I am not stupid. I know that I am in Florida, and now I must find this place and do this thing." His tone softened. "Will you help me do this thing, Alicia? I think God has brought you to me to help me do this."

"Yes, I will help you Juan-Jesus. Be patient for a minute and let me talk to the others."

Alicia turned her attention to the rest of the table. "Well, that's the story. I know we could get Juan-Jesus tested to see if he is a match for his sister. Then, if he is a match, the marrow sample would have to be taken from him in a clinic or doctor's office. Apparently they usually take the marrow from the back of the pelvic bone. I'm told it hurts for a while, but it's a small price to pay. That might be complicated though, since he's in the country illegally and all. Then, if he was a match, I don't know how we could get his sister and him together. Oh, boy, this seems like an impossible task."

Pastor John spoke. "Maybe not, Alicia. Let's take it before the Lord in prayer. He obviously has brought this young man to us for a purpose. Perhaps he has a plan to make all this happen. You folks know as well as I do that there is awesome power in prayer."

"Alicia, would you ask Juan-Jesus if he has spoken to his mother since he left home? Is there any way we can help him do that so she would know that he is OK? Goodness, the poor woman has had a lot to deal with. She must be crazy with worry right now," said Martha.

Alicia nodded and spoke in Spanish to Juan-Jesus. She translated his reply. "No, he says they don't have a phone, but if we call Pastor Rojas he'll get a message to Juan-Jesus's mom and tell her that he is all right. He says he left her a note, and he knows that she is praying for him. He also says she might be just a little worried."

Bear spoke, "Alicia, why don't you do this, being as you speak the language and all. Maybe you could contact Pastor Rojas. Do you know how to reach him?"

"Yes, I can get the number from our church in San Francisco. I can ask them to pray as well. No, wait, Juan-Jesus has his number right here." Alicia replied as she looked over the papers in the backpack.

Bear reached in his pocket and pulled out a handset. "You can use our cell phone to call him. Maybe you could call him right now. He might be able to tell us a little more about what's going on."

Alicia spoke to Juan-Jesus. "How about if I call Pastor Rojas and tell him you're OK so he can tell your mama? I can do that with this phone right here. What do you think?"

"Yes, that would be OK. Please tell him to tell my mama that I'm OK and everything will be just fine. Tell her that I am doing my best to take care of them."

Alicia dialed the numbers and waited for what seemed like a long time before finally getting a connection. Then Pastor Rojas answered the phone.

"Hi Pastor Rojas, this is Alicia Chen. Do you remember me from San Francisco?" Pastor Rojas did remember, and he was delighted to hear that Juan-Jesus was safe and among friends. He promised to get word to Juan-Jesus's mother as soon as possible.

Alicia then asked him some questions about Angelica. Yes, the little girl did indeed have leukemia and was undergoing chemotherapy. But she hadn't responded very well to the treatment. The clinic in Mexicali was not well funded and wasn't up on the latest treatment methods, but the doctors were doing their best. That was about the extent of Pastor Rojas's information. Then he asked if he could talk to Juan-Jesus. Alicia handed Juan-Jesus the phone. They talked briefly, but it was mostly one-sided—Pastor Rojas talked and Juan-Jesus listened. Then Juan-Jesus bowed his head and closed his eyes as Pastor Rojas prayed for him.

The group around the table maintained a respectful silence. Juan-Jesus handed the phone back to Alicia and she turned it off. His face was very serious, and he looked very old for his thirteen years.

Alicia asked him if he was OK.

He forced a smile. "Yes, I am OK, Alicia. I just have much to think about."

Everyone listened as Alicia translated, then Bear spoke. "A little less than two years ago one of our major team owners was diagnosed with a form of leukemia, and it gave the National Bone Marrow Program a big publicity boost. NASCAR kinda took the thing on and did everything they could to bring it in front of the public. One thing that we found is that there is a lot of misinformation out there. Some folks think being a donor is a big deal. Nearly all of the teams got on board and really supported the program, and as a result we got some things straightened out. The test itself is simple. They just take a blood sample and determine the HLA, or the human leukocyte antigen. Taking a blood sample is fairly easy. Then the results go into a computer. You know, they've had over two million donors and four thousand transplants so far, and every day they're doing a little more research. Once they match a donor and recipient, the donor goes in for a clinical procedure, like you said, Alicia, to obtain the marrow. It isn't too bad. One of NASCAR's announcers for a media network, Jerry Punch, is also a doctor. He explained the procedure to us. They usually do it with a local anesthetic and a special needle, but it doesn't take too long. The donor is sore for a few days, but it's a small price to pay for someone to overcome the disease. After they get the marrow, they reduce it to serum and inject it into the recipient. Once it hits the bloodstream, it starts producing what the body needs to fight the disease."

Pastor John and Martha nodded. They both knew about the procedure and, like the whole Orly Mann Racing Team, were registered donors.

Alicia looked around the table. "So, what do you think we should do?"

"Well," said Bear, "I know it sounds kind of small in the grand scheme of things, but we do have the biggest race of the year to run tomorrow. I have some ideas about how we might make some things happen, but I don't think we can do much before Monday."

"Why don't I take Juan-Jesus home with me? I have to get back this morning or my Aunty Grandmothers are going to be very upset. I can make some phone calls and see what we can do. Then Bear, maybe you could have Paolo call me this evening to see what's up?"

"That'll work, Alicia," replied Bear. "In the meantime I'll do some checking with some folks here and see what we can come up with." Bear already had some ideas in the back of his mind. "Alicia, would you do something for me? Would you tell Juan-Jesus that we have the greatest respect for him and what he's doing for his sister. You might tell him that I'm sure his papa would be very proud of him."

Alicia translated Bear's words for Juan-Jesus. He listened carefully, then bowed his head and muttered, *"Gracias, Señor Bear."*

There was silence for a minute, then Bear looked over at the buffet table, which was practically groaning beneath the weight of a multitude of delicious breakfast items. He stood up and patted Juan-Jesus on the shoulder. "Come on, my friend, time to *comer.*"

An hour later, Paolo was standing behind a mock pit wall at the Daytona shop dripping with sweat while he held the special seventeen-pound jack. He carefully fixed his eyes on the backup car at the end of the driveway. It was the Rockingham car and was being driven by one of the crew members. The pit wall might be fake, but it matched the dimensions of the pit wall at the track, and Paolo would be doing this for real tomorrow. The lines on the asphalt were identical too; they measured out the exact size of a pit stall on pit road. The car came rumbling down the pavement and slid to a stop precisely on the white horizontal line. Paolo was ready to time his motions to correspond to the stop of the car. Bud's voice hollered in his ear, "Now!"

Paolo was over the wall as the car rolled to a stop and went flying around the corner of the car to the right side. In one motion, the jack slid under the chassis at the spot marked by a yellow arrow, then Paolo gave a mighty downward push. The car lifted into the air. He gave it another half push just to make sure it was high enough, then he heard Bud's voice through the radio headset.

"Get a feel for it, Paolo. You don't want me and Bobby to have to chase the lug nuts up and down. Try to use only one push on the jack. Now when the tires come off, we're going to lay them right at your feet, so be careful. Make sure they're down flat, but also make sure you always have one hand on the jack. Now you have to drop the jack, clear me, and make sure you don't trip over the air hose. I'll be on my knees, and as soon as you go by I'll be hot on your tail. Slap that jack under the left side and up we go. Be sure to watch your footing. The lug nuts will be flying all over the place, so keep your focus." Bud's constant advice filled Paolo's head. He didn't have a mouthpiece, only earphones, so all he could do was nod. He felt a little like one of those toy dogs in the rear car window that has a spring for a neck.

The rest of the Thunderfoot Ballet Company were assembled with Bud, and they were watching Paolo with critical eyes. Tyrone had been a good jackman, and even though what Bud and Bear said went, they still needed to make up their own minds. Besides, there was more than just a race at stake—there was a whole lot of pride.

Every year NASCAR organized a pit-crew competition at Rockingham Raceway sponsored by Unocal 76. The crews competed against each other, and the winners not only got a little prize money but beautiful championship rings as well. That was nice. But to the Ballet Company, what really counted was that the winning crew had their names painted on the side of the hauler with the recognition that they were the fastest crew in the Winston Cup. It was something to boast about and gave them just a little bit of swagger. Last year the Ballet Company finished first by two thousandths of a second, and they wanted that recognition again this year.

Paolo dropped the jack, and the car accelerated away to circle the building and get ready to do it again. Paolo picked up the jack and stepped back over the wall. He said nothing. He was keeping his mouth shut like Bear told him, and he was listening carefully to everybody and anybody. This was the most exciting thing to happen to him in his whole life, and he didn't want to blow it. Just think—a few months ago he was part of the world of racing fans, and now he was a genuine jackman for the Orly Mann Racing Team. *I hope I don't blow this,* Paolo thought.

"All right, Paolo, I think you got it. Now let's do a few with everybody working together," said Bud. The other men on the crew unfolded their arms and took their places—air guns, tires, and gas cans at the ready. "You ready, Doug?" asked Bud.

"I'm ready, Dad," said Doug, holding up his stopwatch.

Bud gave a wave to the car at the end of the lot, and it came rumbling down the pavement. The Thunderfoot Ballet Company jumped into motion.

Another hour later the whole crew was drenched in sweat, but Paolo wasn't complaining. He would do this until he dropped or Bud said enough, whichever came first. After a stop that was nearly a record-setting time, Bud called a halt. "All right guys, good job. I think we'll be fine tomorrow. Paolo, just do your job, and you'll be plenty OK. Let's take a break for lunch, then we need to get back to the track for Happy Hour. No doubt Bear has plenty for us to do."

Paolo was sitting on the edge of the fake pit wall when Ed Grudum, the gas man, walked up to him and put a hand on his shoulder.

"You'll do, Paolo, you'll do." Then he turned and walked away.

Paolo grinned. He was both pleased and surprised. It wasn't what Ed said that made him smile. It was the fact that Ed had used his name. Paolo was no longer known as Fumbles and, for now, had been accepted as part of the team. *Please, Lord, don't let me screw up tomorrow,* Paolo prayed silently.

The old Cadillac fired right up when Alicia put the key in the ignition and cranked the starter. She maneuvered the thing out of the parking lot and headed through the traffic back to Orlando. Juan-Jesus was silent for a long time as he looked out the window, then he spoke.

"Alicia."

"Yes, Juan-Jesus, what is it?"

"It's a good day to be alive, isn't it?"

"Yes, Juan-Jesus, it is a good day to be alive."

"Alicia, do you think that it hurts to die?"

"Juan-Jesus, why are you asking such a question? What are you thinking about?"

Juan-Jesus didn't answer her question right away. Instead he said, "My papa died and he knew Jesus. When I die at least I will be with my papa, won't I, Alicia?"

Alicia took the next available exit ramp and pulled over on the shoulder of the road. There was something heavy going on here, and she couldn't drive this big car and talk seriously at the same time. She shut the motor off and turned to face Juan-Jesus, sitting beside her in the over-stuffed seat. "Juan-Jesus, what is going on in your head? You're scaring me with this kind of talk. Tell me what you're thinking."

"If they need my blood to make Angelica well, then I will die when they take it. You know, a person cannot live without blood, and I am just thinking what it will be like to die," he said with a shrug of his shoulders.

"Juan-Jesus, do you really think that in order for Angelica to live, you must give up your own life?"

"Yes," Juan-Jesus replied. "Jesus gave up his life for us that we might live in heaven. So I am willing to give up my life for my sister."

"In the first place you are not Jesus. His sacrifice on the cross was once for all who profess him as Savior. Second, Jesus was and is God. Third . . . Juan-Jesus, they will just take a little bit of your blood. It won't hardly even hurt and you won't even notice it. Then they will test it to see if you are a match. You might be, or you might not have the right type of blood so you won't be. Even if you are, then they will just take a little bit of your bone marrow—

the stuff inside your bones—and when they do that it won't hurt for very long. Juan-Jesus, you won't die." Alicia was stunned to think that Juan-Jesus was willing to give up his life for his sister. It was amazing that he had been so willing to leave home and come all the way across the United States. "Juan-Jesus, do you understand what I am saying to you? You misunderstood. What a wonderful sacrifice you were willing to make . . . but you don't have to."

Juan-Jesus looked at Alicia with big eyes. "I don't?" he asked. "Are you sure, Alicia?"

"Yes, Juan-Jesus, I'm positive."

Juan-Jesus's eyes suddenly overflowed with tears. Then he looked away. "I guess I am very happy that I do not have to die, but I am also very sad. I wanted to see my papa."

"Juan-Jesus, you will see your papa some day. In the meantime your mama and both your sisters need you very much. Especially your mama, I think. It's important that you be strong for them all. OK?"

Alicia dug in her purse and handed him a tissue. Juan-Jesus blew his nose, then looked at Alicia. "Thank you for being my friend."

Alicia blew her own nose and started the car. "Come on, let's go to my Aunty Grandmothers' house."

"You mean your aunts' house or your grandmothers' house?" asked Juan-Jesus. "You're using both words in Spanish."

"Actually, Juan-Jesus, they are both my aunts and my grandmothers, and it is a long story . . . let me tell you about it."

It is not good to have zeal without knowledge, nor to be hasty and miss the way.

Proverbs 19:2

"We'll be a dark horse. I'd rather be a dark horse than a favorite."

Team owner Felix Sabates

THE TENSION at the racetrack seemed to blow through the air like discarded hot-dog wrappers caught in the afternoon breeze. It was the so-called Happy Hour, which meant that it was the last practice before the Daytona 500. Some called it the storm before the lull. For nearly two weeks, events had been leading to the race tomorrow, and nerves were at the breaking point. More than one team had to separate driver and crew chief as they argued over setups. The fast teams were feeling cautious optimism mixed with a deep sense of anxiety about what could and most probably would go wrong tomorrow. They were careful during this practice session. More than one car had been destroyed just before the race. Teams that were slow and in need of speed were equally anxious and doing everything they could to discover that last ounce of power during the practice session. They were the ones letting it all hang out and scaring the beans out of crews and other drivers. The garage area looked like an anthill as the race cars came rumbling in off the track and the crews made frantic changes and adjustments. The media were having a field day keeping track of lap times and making predictions based on so-called educated inside information garnered from every source possible.

In contrast, the Orly Mann Racing Team was a sea of tranquility. Orly had taken the car out and run it hard for about ten laps, then brought it in and parked it. It was sitting up on jackstands with the wheels off as the crew meticulously checked every nut and bolt. Orly was standing next to Bear in front of the tool chest. They were trying to converse in low tones over the bedlam in the garage bays.

"Whatta ya think, Bear?"

"I'm happy with it if you are, Orly. I think our testing is payin' off. You're right in lettin' us make it more stable in the handling department. We sacrifice a little bit of speed, but since you gotta come through the whole pickin' pack to get to the front anyway, we gotta give you something to work with."

"Yeah, you ought to see some of those guys going down the back chute. They look like streamers blowing in the wind. Makes me nervous just following them. Some of them want you to draft with them, but I tell you, Bear, if I snugged up and took the air off them they would be in the wall big time. I won't be surprised if they aren't fishing cars out of Lake Lloyd tomorrow." Lake Lloyd sat nearly in the infield and was a long way from the racing surface. It was also protected by a large berm.

"Well, you just be careful, Orly. It's a long race. Stay out of trouble if you can. You and I both know a bunch of these guys are going home on the flatbed tow trucks."

"Yeah, I will. How'd Paolo do in the practice this morning?" asked Orly, changing the subject.

"Bud said he did just fine and that he'll be good during the race. Said he's quick. He also said the other boys are starting to accept him. He's playin' it smart and keepin' his mouth shut and doin' what he's told. I told you he was a good boy."

"I believe you, Bear. Hey, have you seen Tyrone?"

"Yeah, I saw him this morning and we talked for a while," said Bear.

"Yeah, the man had a lot of pent-up stuff inside him. After you left we must've talked till way in the morning. I don't know what time it was when Tyrone went home, but when I got up he was gone. I just wondered if you'd seen him today."

"Yeah, like I said, I saw him. Then he left and said he had some stuff to take care of."

The conversation was interrupted by yet another media team coming through the garage to do an interview. Both

Bear and Orly put their media faces on and said all the proper things, being careful to acknowledge sponsors, with a special thanks to NASCAR for offering such a gargantuan purse. They exchanged looks as the media team sought out other victims.

"We'll meet for supper with Jimmy and Bud tonight as usual, Bear, and discuss strategy. That is, if we got any," said Orly with a laugh. "The truth is, we got no place to go but forward, starting dead last like we are."

Bear winced and wiped his hands on the shop rag. "Yep, see ya then."

The rest of the ride home for Alicia and Juan-Jesus was much happier. An animated Juan-Jesus fiddled with the radio, and he seemed more relaxed to Alicia. The Juan-Jesus Alicia and Paolo knew was a funny guy with an impish sense of humor. Alicia had only seen flashes of that, but once he discovered he wasn't going to die his old personality returned.

They laughed about old times in Mexicali, and Juan-Jesus said it made perfectly good sense to him that Alicia should have three Aunty Grandmothers and he was excited to meet them. He also seemed willing to lay down the burden of Angelica for a time and let Alicia do what she could to help the situation. Finally, they arrived in Orlando, and Alicia pulled the old Caddy into the driveway. She breathed out a sigh of relief at having finally gotten the old horse back to the barn.

Alicia sat in the car catching her breath and collecting her thoughts. As soon as she opened the door she would face a three-pronged barrage of questions, and she had better be ready with answers.

Juan-Jesus waited for her lead and sat quietly in the front seat until she was ready.

Using both hands, she threw open the car door and slid her feet to the ground. "OK, Juan-Jesus, let's do it."

She was right. All three of the Aunty Grandmothers were waiting at the door, and all three began asking questions at the same time in rapid-fire, high-pitched Chinese. The questions to Alicia were mixed with statements to each other like, "Well, she looks OK. Do you think she looks OK? Alicia, are you OK? Where have you been really? Why didn't you try to come home? You should plan better so that your dear old Aunty Grandmothers would not have to worry themselves all night. None of us slept at all last night—we were just worried to death. Shame on you for making us worry so."

Alicia didn't even try to answer them at first, but instead gave the dear old ladies a chance to run down like a wind-up alarm clock. Finally they ran out of noise, and Alicia stepped aside to introduce Juan-Jesus. He stood solemnly with his hands at his side, blinking his eyes. He was not certain just what to think of these little Chinese ladies who all seemed to speak at the same time in a language that was completely foreign to him. They stared back at him. Finally one of them reached out and gently pinched Juan-Jesus's cheek.

"He is very thin, Alicia. Has he come from a poor home?"

Alicia responded, "Yes, he has come a long way and is trying to do something that will save his sister's life."

She then proceeded to tell them Juan-Jesus's story, where he had come from, what he had done, and why he was here. After listening carefully to Alicia's story, the grandmothers pushed her aside and surrounded Juan-Jesus. They spoke in Chinese to each other. "He must be a very brave boy to do all that," said one.

"Yes, very brave," said another. "I think he comes from a poor home, but there is no shame in that. We came from a poor home to a very strange country where people spoke a very strange language. Remember how hard it was for us to get used to the different people and their ways?"

"The thing I remember most was how everything smelled so different here in this country. Do you suppose he notices that?"

Finally the third and oldest Aunty Grandmother spoke. "I am sure he is hungry. Ladies, where are our manners? Let's feed him and make him comfortable."

There was a chorus of agreement, and the next thing Juan-Jesus knew he was being pampered to the point of embarrassment. A half hour later he was sitting at the dining room table absolutely stuffed when Alicia walked into the room, brushing her long black hair.

"Are you still hungry, Juan-Jesus?" she asked.

"No, Alicia, I am not hungry anymore and I do not think I will ever be hungry again. These Aunty Grandmothers of yours can sure cook."

"Yes, they can certainly do that all right." Alicia's comments were interrupted by the telephone.

A minute later one of the grandmothers came out of the kitchen with the phone. "It's a man and he says he wants to talk with you. Do you want to talk with him?"

Alicia took the phone.

"Hello."

"Hello, Alicia. You don't know me, but I know Paolo and Bear and Orly Mann. My name is Tyrone Wallace. I have a couple of things to tell you, but I have to do something first. Do you have that young Mexican boy there with you?"

Alicia wasn't sure how to answer but decided that honesty would be best. She said a quick prayer first. "Yes, you mean Juan-Jesus. Yes, he is here."

"May I speak to him?"

"Yes, but you know he doesn't speak hardly any English. Do you speak Spanish?"

"Well, yes and no. I mean, no. But I have been rehearsing what I want to say to him. It will only take a minute. Please, Alicia." The man sounded sincere. Alicia spoke to Juan-Jesus at the table.

"Juan-Jesus, there is a man on the phone who wants to speak to you." She handed the phone to Juan-Jesus.

He took it and listened. Then he said, "OK," and handed the phone back to Alicia. He whispered to her, "All he said was that his name is Tyrone and he is sorry. He said, '*Lo siento.*' I don't think he speaks any Spanish."

Alicia put the phone to her ear. "Yes."

"Will you please explain to Juan-Jesus that I am the guy who drove the truck and trailer from California. I said some very stupid, prejudicial things to him in a restaurant about being a Mexican and about Mexicans in general. I was mad at him for stowin' away in the trailer and makin' me look bad. I feel very bad, and God has been dealin' with me about my attitudes toward other people.

I just felt like I had to say that I was sorry to him, and I hope he will forgive me. I was pretty stupid and I'm sorry." Tyrone's voice was strained with emotion.

"Do you want me to ask him if he's willing to forgive you?" Alicia asked.

"Please."

Alicia turned to Juan-Jesus. "This is the guy who drove the truck and trailer." Before she could go on, Juan-Jesus's eyes widened in fear.

"You mean the big gringo?" he asked.

"Yes. But listen, Juan-Jesus. He wants to ask for your forgiveness for what he said to you. That's why he said he was sorry. He said God is working on his heart."

"Oh. I guess so, Alicia. I mean, it is what Jesus would want me to do, isn't it?"

"Yeah, it sure is, Juan-Jesus."

"Tell him, sure I forgive him." Then he said, "It ain't no big thang," in perfect English just like Paolo and Doug would say it, and threw both hands up in a palms-out gesture just like they would.

Alicia smiled and covered a giggle.

"Yes, he forgives you, Mr. Wallace."

Tyrone breathed a big sigh of relief. "Now, there's something else. My little boy died from a blood disease similar to what Juan-Jesus's sister has. I talked with Bear, and I understand that the kid has a file of medical records from the Mexican clinic. Is that right?"

"Yes, it is. I don't know what they contain or how extensive they are. I don't understand a lot of the medical Spanish. We were going to see if we could get them translated or read this afternoon. There is bound to be a place in Orlando somewhere."

"Well, listen. When my boy was sick we worked with a doctor at the hospital in Charlotte who was a specialist and worked with, consulted I guess you could say, with other doctors. I called him and explained the situation, and he told me about a Cuban doctor in Orlando. He's a legitimate guy, and he understands the situation with Juan-Jesus being illegal and all. I called the Cuban doctor, and he has agreed to meet with you guys and go over the files. He can set Juan-Jesus up for a donor match if that's warranted. At any rate, he will go over the files with you for sure and tell you what they say. Have you got a pencil? Here's his address and telephone number." Tyrone read out the doctor's name and his address, then went on. "He will make time to meet with you this evenin', so call him first. He's waitin' for you to call."

"I don't know how to thank you, Mr. Wallace. This is great. At least we are getting the ball rolling. I will call him right now. Thank you."

"Alicia, I'm not much of a prayin' man. In fact, I'm not sure if I really know how to pray, but will you tell Juan-Jesus that I will be praying for him and his sister . . . especially for his sister and his mama. And please tell him again that I'm sorry for being such a jerk. He has a lot of guts to do what he's doing. I should have helped him instead of scarin' him to death. Maybe God will forgive me. I hope so."

"The Bible says that God does forgive you, Mr. Wallace. That's what Jesus is all about. You mustn't lose sight of that. Thanks for your call. We'll get going on this thing right now."

As Alicia hung up the phone, she turned to Juan-Jesus and said, "Hey, buddy, I got great news." She repeated Tyrone's words in Spanish to Juan-Jesus. Then she had to share this turn of events in Chinese, which took a great deal longer. There was much clucking and hand-wringing as the Aunty Grandmothers made the appropriate noises to accent the story.

The race car was put to bed for the night, and the garage area was dark except for the security lights. Bear, Orly, Jimmy, and Bud sat around the table in Orly's motor home drinking coffee over empty plates.

"I got to tell you, Orly, you're gettin' to be a really good cook. That was some of the best pasta salad I have ever eaten, especially with that low-fat dressing," said Bud.

Everyone laughed. It was a standard joke. They always ate the same thing on the Saturday night before a race, and it wasn't pasta salad. It was the best T-bone steaks they could find, usually with mashed or baked potatoes, lots of real butter, and either peas or corn. Maybe broccoli. But Bud was right; it was Orly who cooked and he always did a fine job. The steaks were panfried with onions and mushrooms and done to perfection.

"Well, boys, whatta you think?" asked Bear, picking his teeth with a toothpick. "How's it going to play out?"

"Well, I have a thought," said Jimmy in his slow Texas drawl. "There's been a lot of general crashing and mayhem going on in the other races this week. The Busch race today was a real slaughter. Over a third of the field didn't finish. So I'm thinking that tomorrow morning in the drivers, meeting they're going to give you guys what for. That, plus the fact that most of the Cup guys watched the race today, and they are going to be minding their p's and q's. I betcha the race goes green for sixty to eighty laps, because everybody's going to do their best to stay out of trouble. That's what I think."

The other men around the table nodded their heads in agreement. "Yup, could be," said Bear. "I feel bad, Orly, we got you starting so far back. That seems to be the pattern though. I checked back in the files, and sure enough the first laps are run under green. I suppose the key is going to be to find somebody to draft with."

"Yeah, that's the key," Orly agreed. "I think it's a little funny that the media folks are making such a big deal about guys pairing up to draft. With all the multicar teams, everyone thinks we're playing tennis or something. Drafting is opportunistic. You go with whoever is the fastest and try not to get hung up in the middle or the outside. I've been watching some of the boys out there, and some of them are very good at drafting, and some of them just scare the pants off you. I'm glad that we have set the car up stable, like we said. I'm willing to sacrifice a little flat-out speed to get the thing to work better in the draft. What's the weather supposed to be like?"

"Well, I went by the weather station at NASCAR, and they're predicting a drop in temperature and maybe a little overcast. I'll be up early, and I won't jet the carb until just before we push the car out on the pit lane," said Bear.

"You know, Orly, if it stays green a long time and we get one, maybe two, green flag stops, the boys will do real well. They're looking good, and at practice this morning they were ripping off some really good numbers. I think we might be able to move you up some if that happens," said Bud.

Orly nodded. "Yeah, I expect so. The Thunderfoot Ballet Company is the best there is." Then he turned to Jimmy.

"I'm going to really be relying on you, Jimmy. We have a good car. Actually, I think it's better than a good car. I think if we can get to the front, we can run with them up there. Getting there is going to be the tough part. It's so pickin' easy to get caught up in something in the back or the middle of the pack. Most of the guys running there are there because their cars aren't any better or they can't drive any better. It makes it kind of scary. I'm going to have to pick and choose, and you're going to have to help me out a big bunch."

"Yeah, I know, Orly, and we'll do our best," said Jimmy. "It's a lot like wearing a three-piece suit while driving a manure spreader. I mean, we're all dressed up with a fast car, and we should be at the dance with the other good-lookers. Instead, we're out in the field with the other tractors. It really is too bad we have to start last. And dead last to boot." Jimmy was famous for mixing his metaphors.

The conversation went on as these veterans discussed various scenarios. They were experienced men and had been in nearly every situation possible in the course of a Winston Cup race.

Orly spoke, "Well, boys, I have one question. Are we going to run this race to just finish and stay out of trouble, or are we going to run this race to win? Personally, I think we got the iron to win tomorrow. What do you think? It's the first race of the season, the points are important, and the purse is out of sight."

Bear summed it up both ways, "Orly, we only race one way and that is to win. You know that. You taught us. But you know that sixty-four of the last eighty winners of the Daytona races have come from the top ten. Ain't nobody ever won this race any farther back than thirtieth or something, and for sure ain't nobody ever won the thing starting dead last!"

Everybody laughed out loud. "Well, why the heck not start something new!" said Jimmy. "Boy, howdy, we'd have to beat the TV and radio folks off with a stick. What a party that would be!"

"So, it's decided then. We're going to do our best to win the thing," said Orly. The table was quiet as the other three men nodded their heads in assent. "All right then. I only have one more question. Who wants some nonfat ice cream with a little chocolate cake on the side?"

Paolo and Doug, along with some of the other crew braved the Daytona Saturday night crowds and went out for pizza. It was tenish when they got back to the motor home. There was a note from Bear lying on Paolo's bunk. He read it, then quickly jumped in the air, shouting. "Aw right, great!"

Doug was sitting on his bunk and looked up with a question in his eyes. Paolo handed him the note and streaked toward the door. "Here. Read this," he said over his shoulder, "I gotta go call her."

Five minutes later Paolo was ensconced at the pay phone talking to one of the Aunty Grandmothers.

"Yes, ma'am, it's me, Paolo. Yes, Pally. No, I didn't make her stay out all night. No, I wouldn't do that. There were a lot of things going on . . . No . . . No. OK, I'm sorry. OK, I'll wait."

A few minutes later Alicia came to the phone. "Hey, Pally, so you got the third degree. You know how it is. They love me too much to get mad at me, so they get mad at you. So what's new with you? I got tons of news for you."

"Hey, Alicia, it's good to hear your voice. I'm sorry I missed you this morning. I'm glad you got home OK. So, you tell me your news first and then I'll tell you mine."

"Well, we got a call from Tyrone not too long after we got home. You know, Pally, he was really broken up. At any rate, he talked to Juan-Jesus and told him he was sorry for being so mean and prejudicial to him and all. Then he set it up for us to meet with this doctor to go over the medical charts that Juan-Jesus had in his backpack."

"Yeah, Bear told me he had a bunch of stuff in there."

"Well, this doctor was very nice and he spoke kindly to Juan-Jesus. He has set up an appointment with a special clinic in San Diego, and they are going to make arrangements for Juan-Jesus's mom and both his sisters to come across the border. I'm flying back with him in—guess what—Orly Mann's airplane on Monday after the race. Bear and Orly set it all up."

"Whoa, big time, Alicia."

"Yeah, Juan-Jesus can hardly believe it himself. Anyway, they'll run tests to see if Angelica is suitable for a recipient program and get them hooked up with the donor program. Judging from what this doctor says, Juan-Jesus probably has the best chance of being a donor. Once they get everyone to the clinic, they'll sort it all out."

"Man, that's neat, Alicia. God really has answered some prayers on this thing, hasn't he?"

"Yes, he has, Pally. We're still praying that Angelica will get what she needs to fight this disease."

"Well, how would you and Juan-Jesus like to come to the race tomorrow?"

Alicia squealed with excitement. Then her tone hardened. "Pally, that would be great, but I don't know how we could possibly do that. The traffic is murder. We would've had to leave two hours ago just on the off chance we might get there before it started."

"Hey, girl, you forget who you're talking to. I'm the jackman for the Orly Mann Racing Team and I have connections. Well, at least somebody has connections. The sponsor helicopter is picking up some folks at the Orlando airport tomorrow morning at eight o'clock, and they have two extra spots reserved for you and Juan-Jesus. They will land in the infield, and Orly's publicist, Helen, will meet you guys and give you your passes. You can watch the race from the hauler with Doug or from the VIP grandstand. Whatever you want."

Alicia squealed again, this time with laughter. "Wow, Pally. That's great! I'm so excited. I can't tell you how it made me feel to be at the track and know that I'd have to watch the race and you on TV."

"Hey, don't thank me. You have to thank Bear and Orly."

"Pally, are you nervous?"

"Listen, Alicia, you're my friend, and I tell you stuff I don't tell anybody else, right?"

"Right, that's 'cause you trust me, Pally, because you know I really care about you."

Paolo gulped. Alicia's bluntness always made him a little nervous. "Well, Alicia, I'm more scared and shaky than I've ever been in my whole life. I'm so afraid I'm going to screw up big time and do something stupid and cost Orly the race . . ."

Alicia spoke in a quiet, fierce tone, "Listen to me, Pellegrini. You are going to do the best ever job of doing whatever it is that you do on that race car, and the Thunderfoot Ballet Company is going to be the best that it ever was. Mark my words. You're good . . . and don't you forget it."

Paolo laughed at her tone of voice. "Thanks, Alicia. You're the best. So it's settled. I'll try to see you before the race. If not, you know where I'll be. You and Juan-Jesus will have great fun. At any rate, I'll see you after the race."

"Good night, Pally. We'll see you tomorrow." Alicia hung up the phone and said to the air, "I love you, Pally. You need me to encourage you."

Bear and Orly were finishing up the dishes. Bud and Jimmy had gone back to their motor home for the night. As Bear washed, Orly dried.

"So, you got it all set up?" asked Bear.

"Yeah, it wasn't easy. We had to pull a few strings, but with Tyrone's help it came together. I'm going to fly them to San Diego on Monday in the twin. You really don't need me back at the shop until Thursday late, and I could use the break. Oh yeah, in case I get hurt or something, make sure they get on a commercial flight, OK, Bear?"

Bear, like Orly, was a realist. Race car drivers got hurt on occasion. It was part of the business, and Orly had been hurt many times before. His limp was much in evidence tonight.

"Yeah, Orly, I'll take care of it. You know I will."

"You know, I was thinking, Bear. If we can win this thing, I sure would like to buy John and Martha a new motor home. Plus, I got some other things I would like to do. How much do you think it . . . Well, never mind."

"Yeah, that would be nice, but let's win the thing first."

"No good counting our chickens and all that I suppose. Though I got to tell you, I have a funny feeling about this race. This car you got under me is one of the best, if not *the* best, that I have ever had here. You done good, Bear."

"Yeah, well, you know it takes more than just a good car to win here, Orly. I got a feeling about tomorrow's race too, and I think it's going to be a wild and woolly affair."

Ten minutes later, Bear was out the door and Orly was sitting in the overstuffed chair trying to relax. He needed to sleep. He would need all of his strength and stamina tomorrow, but he knew that sleep would not come easy tonight. He looked around the empty confines of the motor home and hungered to hear the echoes of voices long gone. He stretched out his arm and picked up the worn Bible off the counter.

For as churning the milk produces butter, and as twisting the nose produces blood, so stirring up anger produces strife.

Proverbs 30:33

"I'm sure there will be a little bit of butterflies on Sunday morning because it's been a while since we raced. This is the Daytona 500 . . . and that puts the butterflies churning just a little bit."

Larry McReynolds, crew chief, Winston Cup car #31

ORLY WAS INSTANTLY AWAKE. He had been dreaming, but he couldn't recall what the dream was about. At any rate, it was so vivid it made his eyes fly open. It didn't matter anyway—it was only a dream. Dreams didn't count

183

much in the real world. At least not his real world. He took stock of his body and figured he had been asleep for a good six hours, which was OK for him. He glanced at the clock and it agreed with his assessment. He stretched and yawned. He felt relaxed, and that was a good sign. As soon as he acknowledged that he felt relaxed, his stomach began to tighten . . . and that too was a good sign. Maybe today would be the day. Maybe he could pull it off. The ever-elusive Daytona 500. The car seemed good enough, but then again maybe today he would find himself in the infield care center, strapped to a gurney groaning in pain, getting ready for a flight for life to the hospital in the med-evac helicopter. Or worse yet, the car could blow up on the warm-up lap, and he would be done before he started. Anything was possible . . . and most all things were probable, he smiled to himself. He laid in the warmth of the covers for a minute and took stock of his body and his feelings once again. Yeah, there it was. That tiny knot of fear that was way back deep in his consciousness. Just a little nag. It was good to be just a little bit afraid. It kept him from making stupid decisions and getting carried away with himself. He welcomed the fear like an old friend. Yes indeed, it was a day to make war, and he relished the prospect. A day to be a little afraid and brave at the same time. The battle waited, and warriors never felt quite right until they were in battle.

It was a little different in the crew's motor home. For one thing it was a lot noisier. The alarm went off with a clanging that resounded throughout the bunks, eliciting groans and snorts. Bear threw his feet over the edge of his bunk and hit the floor with his mouth running while he scratched and stretched. Bear was a morning person and woe unto the crew guy who wasn't. He almost always woke up cheerful and always was delighted to experience the freshness of yet another sunrise. In Bear's eyes, mornings were the best time of the day, and the earlier the better. He was renown for waking up loud, and this morning he was especially loud. "All right my overpaid beauties. Time to roll out. We got work to do today and hopefully a little money to make as well. Ol' NASCAR has seen fit to give us a shot at a biiiiig pot of gold, and it's a fine day to go racin'. Pastor John has chapel in about twenty minutes for those of us going, then to breakfast and the team meeting. Let's go, guys." Then in the loudest voice he could muster he said, in the fashion that ring announcer Michael Buffer has made famous, "Let's geeeet reaaady to ruuuumble." He was met with another chorus of groans, this time accompanied by dirty socks and underwear.

A while later the crew was finishing breakfast and drinking a third cup of coffee. It was game day and they looked sharp in their uniforms. Orange pants with a yellow stripe and purple thunderbolt up the outside of the leg, and orange shirts set off with broad purple monograms on the back that announced them as the Orly Mann Racing Team. The over-the-wall guys each had a little medallion embroidered in their shirts with purple thread that said "Thunderfoot Ballet Company" right above their names. Paolo kept fingering his, trying not to look down. He kept shaking his head in disbelief. He hadn't slept much and spent most of the night tossing and turning. Today was it and he was scared and incredibly anxious.

Soon it was time for the prerace meeting. Everybody knew the drill. Bear would lay out the strategy for the race and give the team a serious boot of encouragement, telling them how good they were and how much this race meant, and so forth. They were pros and they had been here before. They could all practically say Bear's speech by heart, but it didn't mean that they didn't want to hear it.

Yup, they'd all heard it before . . . except Paolo. His stomach was so knotted he could barely eat breakfast and he was doing his best not to look anxious, but unfortunately it was not a feeling he hid well.

Doug said to him privately. "Hey Pally, listen. Can I give you some advice? You know, from your old friend Doug?"

"Yeah, Doug, talk to me."

"Pally, you're worrying too much about yourself. My dad says if you start thinking just about yourself and forget that you're part of a team, then you'll screw up for sure. So just remember that all of us are working together. OK?"

"Yeah, I hear you, Doug, but what if I do something stupid?"

"Personally, I don't think you're going to do anything stupid. But we could play the 'What if?' game all day. Hey, Paolo, give it over to the Lord and let's have some fun. Just think how exciting today is. Don't spoil your own fun."

"Yeah, I gotcha Doug. Hey, Doug?"

"Yeah?"

"You're starting to sound like Alicia." Both young men laughed and Doug slapped Paolo on the back. It made Paolo feel better. He really could do this, and with the Lord's help he would do it great!

Bear called the team together and, much to everyone's surprise, Tyrone walked up to join the group. Bear motioned to Tyrone and the conversation died down. Tyrone spoke, "Before Bear talks to you guys, I just wanted to say something to you all. I'll make it short. I ain't so good at speeches. As you all know, I got fired. I want you to know that I deserved it because I've been a bit of a jerk these past few months. I call you guys my friends, and I've made it real difficult for you to be around me. I apologize for that. It seems like everythin' just came crashin' down on me. You know that I lost my boy a few years back and then me and my wife are getting a divorce . . . and well, things just got worse from there, and I found myself hatin' the whole world. I thought maybe gettin' away for a while and drivin' the show-car rig would help, but it just made things worse. I did something real stupid when I got drunk and wrecked the team truck. I was too embarrassed to call anybody, but Orly found out and bailed me out. I gotta go to court on Monday and I might go to jail, which ain't no fun." There was a chorus of laughter from the team, which broke the tension a little.

"I'm trying to straighten my life out, and with the help of Pastor John and Orly I think I've found the way to do that. I'm not ready to talk about it yet, but maybe someday I will be. At any rate, I wanted you guys to know I've been a jerk and I wanted to apologize to ya'll. Bear and Orly have been real good to me, and as soon as I get this drunk-drivin' thing handled, Bear said that maybe—and that's a big maybe—I could go back to work at the shop in Charlotte and build cars. We'll see how that works out."

Tyrone shuffled his feet and took his hands out of his pockets.

"Today is special. Ya'll know that. There ain't nothin' like the Daytona Race to get the season off to a good start. I been watchin' the new kid, Paolo, handle the jack, and I think he's gonna do the Ballet Company proud. So I'm just sayin' have a great day guys and maybe I'll see you back in North Carolina." With that, Tyrone sat down.

Bear stood up and gave his usual talk, and everybody listened with half an ear, still digesting Tyrone's words. It was a shock to hear him talk like that. It hadn't been his usual style, and it sure seemed something was working on him, or maybe in him. As the group broke up and got ready to head to the garage area, Tyrone walked up to Paolo.

"Hey, kid. Come here a minute and talk to me."

Paolo stopped and turned to face Tyrone.

"Did you play football?" Tyrone asked.

"Some," said Paolo.

"What position?"

Paolo responded, "Well, I played center and guard, mostly, but I wasn't all that good."

"That's what I thought. I mean, not that you weren't any good, just that you looked like you played a little ball. Listen, do you remember that little half step they probably taught you when you were playing guard and you pulled out on a sweep or a trap block?" asked Tyrone.

"Yeah, the one where you lead with your outside foot with your first step instead of crossing over."

"Well, listen, when you're on the right side of the car and you have to cut back to raise the left side on a four-tire stop, use that little cross step instead of crossing over. It'll save you a tenth or so. Might make the difference," said Tyrone. "Oh, another thing. No matter how hairy it gets in the pit lane, stay focused on your job. If you don't, the other boys could get hurt."

"Hey Tyrone, thanks. That's a good tip and I will stay focused, no matter what," said Paolo, smiling. Then he added, "Tyrone?"

"Yeah."

"Thanks for helping out with Juan-Jesus. Alicia told me what you did. You were an answer to prayer, you know."

"Thanks, kid. I needed to do that. He's a brave kid. Have a good race!" With that, Tyrone turned his back and walked away.

Doug had been watching out of earshot.

"What was that all about?" he asked.

Paolo replied, "I'll tell you later." Paolo grabbed Doug around the waist and lifted him off the ground in exuberance, "Hey Doug, let's go racin'."

There was a different feeling in the garage area this day—a sense of finality in the air. The place was a hotbed of frantic activity. There were twice as many people as on Saturday. People of all shapes and sizes and most of them just plain getting in the way of the crews trying to do their jobs. There was a genuine purpose to the frenzy, though. Today was it. This time tomorrow the place would be deserted, and the Daytona 500 would be yesterday's headlines. All the hard work was done. The only thing left now was to run the race and, in the words of Bear, "Dance with the girl you brung." It was time to check and double-check everything, put it back together, fill it up, seal it off, and go for it.

Bear loved race day and he was having a little fun. He was standing just outside the garage stall sniffing the air while holding the carburetor jet box in his hand. He looked like he was about to make an important decision that could affect his team's chances of winning the race, and he was making a show of it. He looked at the sky and sniffed the air once again, testing the moisture like an old hound dog smelling the moon. He looked down at the box in his hand, which was filled with the small brass jets that metered the fuel into the carburetor. Too fat of a jet and the engine would run rich and burn excess fuel, which translated into lousy mileage and more pit stops. Too lean of a jet could mean a burned piston or two and ultimately a blown motor. He shook the box, rattling the jets, and then opened the lid and rummaged around with a blunt finger. Each jet was the size of a pencil eraser and graduated by the size of the hole in the middle that carried the gasoline. It also sat in a carefully marked slot with a white piece of paper taped to the edge of the box. Bear knew that there were many eyes on him as he examined the box once again. He took a jet out and looked at it, then put it back, shaking his head as if to say, "Naw, not that one today." Paolo was watching him over his shoulder as he organized the tools and got ready to move the war wagon to the pit lane. He said to Doug, "What in the world is Bear doing?"

"Oh, Bear? He's playing, Paolo. He knows some of the other guys are watching him and waiting for him to decide which jets to use. See, look over there. Two guys from the #4 car team are watching him like a hawk. There are probably some other guys around here with binoculars or maybe video cameras trying to scope what he's doing. Watch now. See, he looks like he's trying to decide. You want to know something?"

"What?" Paolo asked.

"He's already decided. In fact, he's already put the ones he's going to use in the carb. He was over at the weather station checking the forecast and the humidity first thing this morning. It's going to be overcast today and that's going to affect mileage. Everyone thinks he just feels in his bones which jets to use, but he doesn't. Orly's cars are known for getting the best fuel mileage in a race without sacrificing any power. Bear's smart and is about as scientific as you can be. He likes to pretend he's just a good ol' boy, but it's just an act. My dad says sometimes Bear gets up in the middle of the night before a race to turn on the satellite TV and check the weather. Now watch. He'll take some bogus ones out of the box, flash them around, and then casually put them in his pocket when he puts the carb together. It's just part of the game, Paolo. Anybody that copies the numbers he's using will either be too fat or lean. Ol' Bear isn't about to tip his hand to anybody." Doug slammed a drawer shut on the tool box and whispered: "Orly says Bear's name should be Fox, like 'smart like a.' He loves this game."

The car was finished and ready for battle. The crew pulled the jackstands and dropped the car to the concrete, where it glittered in the early morning sunshine. Bear and two of the crew pushed the car out of the garage stall and into the tech line for its final inspection before the race. Once it passed through tech, it would be pushed out to the pit lane and covered up. The crew would no longer be able to do any work on the car until the green flag fell. Bear got involved in a conversation with a couple of other crew chiefs getting their cars teched. It wasn't long before all three of them were laughing at each other's outrageous claims about the setups of their cars.

In the meantime, Paolo and the rest of the crew gathered the tools and equipment and made the walk from the garage area to set up shop in the pit stall. Paolo paid close attention as the crew rolled the war wagon into place with all of its assorted accouterments. It was like an oversized cabinet about the size of a Volkswagen and was beautifully painted in the team colors. Underneath the bright exterior was a high-tech, complicated piece of equipment. It had built-in computer connections with a monitor set so Bear could see it. There was also a TV monitor that was connected to a satellite receiver so the crew could watch the network TV feed of the race. It held the air bottles that powered the guns the crews used to change the tires. It also held the assorted tools and most of the spare parts that might be needed in the heat of battle. On top, there were two brackets for padded captain's chairs for Bear and another spotter to watch the race. No one liked to sit up there with Bear because he got a little crazy in his excitement, and a fellow could be black-and-blue before the day was over from being slapped on the back. Bear's perch gave him a bird's-eye view of what was going on up and down the pit lane, but he could seldom stay in the chair for very long.

As Paolo helped pushed the wagon he felt a sudden tingle down his back. He looked at the grandstands across the track and they were—gulp—jam-packed. He suddenly realized that this place was rocking and rolling with thousands and thousands of people. He had been here nearly two weeks and thought he had seen a crowd or two, but it was nothing like today. As they pushed the wagon into place, Paolo turned to see that several photographers were taking his picture at the same time. He nervously wiped his hands. He walked over to Doug and said in his ear, "Man, Doug, I've never seen so many people. I thought Sears Point had a good crowd, but this place is jammed. Every time I turn around, somebody's taking my picture."

Doug laughed. "Forget it, Paolo. Just do the job. You'll get used to it. Remember one thing, though. Don't say anything or give any interviews without asking Bear."

Paolo blushed. "Interviews, oh man, no way. I'm not talking to anybody."

Just about that time a young couple walked up to Paolo.

"Excuse me. Are you a member of the Thunderfoot Ballet Company?" the young man asked.

Paolo thought a minute, then said, "Uh, yeah, I think.... Yes, I'm a member of the Ballet Company."

"Would you sign our program for us, please?" asked the young man, holding out the program with a pen.

Paolo wiped his palms on his pants, took the pen and program, and signed "Paolo Pellegrini" with a flourish. Then he handed the items back.

The young man looked at his signature and said, "You're new to the team, aren't you?"

Paolo responded, "Yeah, I sure am."

The young man looked at him and said, "Well, have a good race. You guys are sure fun to watch. I hope you do good today." Then he put his arm around the girl with him and they went off to find another celebrity.

Paolo shook his head. Ed, the gas man, had been watching the whole thing. He smiled and yelled at him in a good-natured way, "Paolo the celebrity, Paolo the magnificent, Paolo the Thunderfoot Ballet Dancer. Hey, Paolo, don't let me pop your balloon, but we need you to come over here and get your famous hands dirty by helping me 'n Ted stack these tires." Paolo blushed a little as the rest of the guys laughed. Then he smiled and yelled back, "You guys are just jealous, that's all. You're just jealous because I'm young and handsome."

The good-natured kidding was on full-time, and it was a way of breaking the tension.

Finally the pit stall was carefully put together with the air hoses coiled and every tool in its special place, to Bud's satisfaction. Ted, the tire man, stacked his tires with Ed and Paolo according to a well-thought-out plan. Daytona was relatively easy on tires in terms of wear, but pressure adjustments could make a lot of difference. Ted and Bear had spent a lot of time with their heads together with the Goodyear people. This day it would not be unusual for Orly to go through six or maybe seven sets of tires. At more than $350 apiece, that was a large chunk of change.

A few minutes later, Bear and the other crewmen emerged from the tech shed and pushed the car down the driveway into the pit lane. Paolo stepped over the pit wall to help them. Bear looked over at him and gave him a big wink. "You ready to go racin', Paolo?"

"Yessir, Mr. Bear, I am."

They rolled the car to the end of the long line ahead of them. *Orly has his work cut out for him,* thought Paolo as he looked over the tops of the race cars that were ahead of them. *That's a lot of iron to get around.* He helped cover the car and walked back to the pit stall just in time to see Alicia and Juan-Jesus walk up. She waved at him and he waved back, smiling. He looked more closely and then laughed out loud. Juan-Jesus was wearing every piece of Orly Mann souvenir paraphernalia possible. He had an orange and yellow cap pulled down around his ears and was wearing an orange Orly Mann Racing Team T-shirt that was slightly too big. It was covered with buttons and pins proclaiming his allegiance to the Orly Mann Racing Team and the Thunderfoot Ballet Company. He even had an oversized Orly Mann belt buckle holding up his jeans. Then, to top off the whole ensemble, he was wearing a pair of sunglasses that gave him a rakish Latin-lover look. He also had a little radio with an earphone stuck in one ear.

"Hey, Alicia, how was the helicopter ride?" asked Paolo.

"It was great, Pally! Juan-Jesus was so excited he could hardly sit still. It was a riot. We got here in nothing flat. When we landed Helen fixed us right up. She gave Juan-Jesus free run of the souvenir stand, and here is the result," said Alicia, pointing at Juan-Jesus.

"What's he listening to on the radio?"

"Oh, he's found the Spanish broadcast of the race, so he's getting right into the thick of things."

Juan-Jesus spied Paolo and gave him a big wave and a smile. "Hello, Paolo," he said in heavily accented English. "I listen to the race."

Bear walked up and examined Juan-Jesus with his hands on his hips. "I think you got it pretty well covered there, Señor Zorro."

Juan-Jesus did a slow turn for everyone to see and then made a little bow. He said in English, "I Señor race fan of Orly Mann."

The tension broke a little as everyone laughed.

"Come on, Zorro, we have to get over to the transporter and help Doug," said Alicia. Then she motioned for Paolo to come closer. She whispered in his ear, "Stop fretting. You're going to do fine, Pally." Then she quickly kissed his cheek and walked away.

Paolo flushed a little. The coolness of her lips lingered on his skin, and he reached up to feel where her lips touched him.

Juan-Jesus looked at him over his shoulder and gave him a big smile, as he patted his heart, making the universal pitter-pat sign. Paolo waved back at him with a gesture that said, "Forget it, pal, she's not interested in me."

Paolo turned around to see Bear looking at him. "What are you looking at, Señor Bear?" he asked.

Bear responded, "Oh, nothing. Nothing at all, lover boy."

Orly was sitting on a folding chair in the media center at the mandatory drivers' meeting. Miss the drivers' meeting and start at the back of the pack—that was the rule. *As if it matters to me today,* thought Orly. They were getting the usual lectures about pit lane speeds and jumping the restarts, but there were also some very stern words about taking foolish chances. The day would be overcast, and the wind would pick up off the ocean as the race progressed into the afternoon, which could make running close together a little hairy. Of course, everybody knew that if you were going to stay in the draft and stay hooked up, you had to run together no matter what the wind was doing.

Orly looked around the room and easily spotted the drivers in the mixed crowd. They were the ones who had that sort of detached, faraway look in their eyes. He wondered mildly if he had that look as well. *Yeah, probably.* Finally the meeting came to a close with a benediction and the exhortation that "you are the best drivers in the world, so act like it and make everyone proud of NASCAR." Orly smiled and joked as he made his way through the crowd back to his motor home to suit up. He stopped on occasion to sign an autograph and even had his picture taken with several fans. Finally, he reached the solace of his motor home.

Orly jumped in the shower for a quick wash and then took his time suiting up. Sometimes he liked to be alone before a race and sometimes he didn't. It depended on his mood. He knew the minute he stepped out the door in his driver's suit with his helmet bag, he would be scrutinized by thousands of people. He slipped into the one-piece suit that was his walking billboard and sat quietly on the edge of the bed. Finally, he put on his flameproof socks and went through his helmet bag to make sure he had what he needed. He stood up in front of the mirror and combed his hair. The back of his hands and the burned spot on his neck were healing nicely. He held his hands out in front of him and studied them for a minute. Yup, they were shaking a little bit. "Probably drank too much coffee this morning," he said out loud. Then he laughed and sat on the edge of the bed to put on his special flameproof, custom-made, high-top driver's shoes, making sure that every lace was straight. He finished dressing and looked at himself in the mirror once again, smiled a crooked smile, grabbed the helmet bag, and stepped out into the multitude.

It was getting close to race time. The drivers had been introduced, and the local dignitaries made their little speeches. Jimmy stood on top of the building with the rest of the spotters, listening to a popular music star sing the national anthem. As he belted out the finale, the four F-16s from Pensacola did a low-level flyby, making the crowd duck. Jimmy noted mildly that he could just about see straight across into the cockpit of the nearest plane. Then, in a thunder of sound, they were gone. Jimmy put the binoculars to his eyes and watched Orly slip his body through the netted window. The rest of the crew had been standing in a long line out from their pit stall with their caps over their hearts during the national anthem. But now they were moving over the wall. Bear stayed next to the car—he would stay there until the motor was running, just in case. NASCAR was beginning to run the media off the pit lane, and it wouldn't be long now.

Bear put his head in the window and helped Orly with the straps of the seat-belt harness. "I think we're ready, Orly. I don't know what else we can do."

"We're ready, Bear. Tell the boys I need every break I can get. Listen, Bear, I've been thinking. If it stays green a while, I'm going to let it all hang out and make some moves to the front as quick as I can. I think we're a lot faster than most of these guys in the back, so I'm going to go for it. What do you think?"

As if it matters, thought Bear. "Just remember, five hundred miles is a long way, Orly. Do what the car will let you do. No more, no less." Then Bear put his hand on Orly's shoulder and prayed quickly, "Lord, keep my friend Orly safe today, and let us all be a good witness for you."

A disembodied voice came booming over the loudspeakers.

"Gentlemen, start your engines . . ."

Orly reached over and flicked on the red switches, then pushed the starter button. The engine blasted to life as if it was eager to get this show on the road. Orly looked over at Bear and gave him a thumbs-up. Bear gave him a final pat, and Orly snapped the window netting into place. He was eager too.

When the righteous thrive, the people rejoice; when the wicked rule, the people groan.

Proverbs 29:2

"We will work with whoever we can to get to the front, then it's every man for himself."

Dale Jarrett, driver, Winston Cup car #88

THE CROWD WAS on its feet as the pace car came around for the third and final lap. Like a rabbit heading for a hole, it ran for cover down the pit lane and out of harm's way. The honorary starter, who was an NFL quarterback, waved the green flag with one hand and tried to cover his ears with the other as he unleashed the pack of forty-three screaming cars. He was immediately hustled out of the starter's box as the pack came thundering by in a cacophony of sound that shook stomachs and made conversation, and even clear thinking, impossible. The Great American Race was on.

For Orly the start was less than dramatic. It would take at least two laps for things to sort themselves out, and he was stuck at the tail end. No sense in getting eager until the car was ready—then he would implement his plan. He checked his gauges as the field began to string out. By the end of the first lap, he could feel the tires warming up and the pace beginning to quicken. As the second lap concluded and he flashed by the starter's box, he clicked the mike twice. It was his signal to Jimmy that he was getting antsy and was ready to move. He moved to the inside and went by two cars with sheer power before the opening closed up ahead of him.

Jimmy's voice spoke in his ear. "It looks like a parade, Orly. Everybody's minding their business for now. The 7 car is two cars ahead of you, and he might make a dancing partner if you can get there." Orly clicked the mike button twice. He picked off another car as he swept down the banking in turn four and sailed down the dogleg. He could see the 7 car ahead of him. Going into turn one, he ducked to the inside of another car and eased up behind the 7 car. He saw the driver wave his hand in the follow-me motion and Orly snuggled up next to his bumper. The car he'd just passed eased in behind him, and the three-car draft was in motion.

The more cars that ran in a straight line, the quicker the draft became. The front car was pushing the air and it created a vacuum behind it. The second car pulled into the vacuum, and the force pushing the front car through the air was increased. When six cars got hooked up, everybody was flying like the midnight freight through Georgia. Of course, the disadvantage was that guys were getting into the corners sometimes a lot quicker than they wanted to, and not everybody's car was handling good enough to stay hooked up. It was a quick way to separate the fast from the "not so fast."

Orly changed partners as circumstances dictated. He drafted with a guy until he was in position to get by and move up a notch. The classic move was to duck down low going into a corner and force the lead car up the track and then take the lead. It had to be done with precision, and all the while hoping that the guy behind him would follow when he made the pass. If nobody followed Orly into the pass, he would find himself on the inside without a partner and then would have to fall back into line.

The first ten laps went fast. *Only 190 to go,* Bear thought. Right now there was nothing to do but watch. The fuel and tire window wouldn't open until at least lap fifty. As long as the flag was green, there wasn't anything to do but race. The laps continued.

Jimmy's voice was getting monotonous as he spoke in Orly's earphone. Orly would come up on a car and Jimmy would say, "Inside." Orly would go inside and Jimmy would say, "Clear," when Orly had made a clean pass.

Orly keyed the mike. "Talk to me, Doug."

Doug was ready. Alicia was sitting on a stool next to him with earphones. Juan-Jesus was hanging onto the rail, listening to the Spanish broadcast with his little radio in his hand.

"There are about twelve cars running in the lead pack, and they've pulled away some. There's a second group of about fourteen cars, and you're just coming up on them. They're running three wide sometimes, and there's some heavy racing going on. Be careful with this bunch, Orly. I've got you in about twenty-fifth; no, twenty-fourth. Only one car is out right now, but a couple are running wounded behind you."

Orly's mike clicked twice.

"How's the car, Orly?" asked Bear when there was a break in the traffic.

"How many laps have we run, Bear?"

Doug answered for him. "Thirty-two."

"I'm just starting to get a little push going in the corner. Maybe put just a little more tape on the grille when we get a chance. Other than that the thing is running great. I really haven't been able to turn it loose completely yet." Then Orly clicked the mike twice. If he had clicked it three times or just once, it would have meant that he was running as fast as he could and couldn't do much more. He was sending the team a message. The fact that other competitors and about a zillion fans were listening on scanners to their radio transmissions made code a necessity sometimes. The bottom line was that Orly still had something in reserve.

Lap forty came and went and still the race stayed green. The same front pack was joined by a group from the second pack, and now seventeen cars were running nose to tail. Orly was only able to move up two more spots and was still four seconds behind the leader's group.

The engine droned in Orly's ears as he laid the car into the first turn once again. He was getting frustrated. He wanted to be up with the leaders, or at least in the front group, but he couldn't get there. He couldn't get the guys behind him to hook up, for whatever reason, and he just didn't have enough power with the choked down restrictor motor to catch them. He would have to be patient. He unconsciously corrected his line with subtle movements of the steering wheel as he blasted off the corner at 190-plus miles per hour.

Lap forty-eight rolled off the counter, then lap fifty. Paolo felt his stomach muscles tighten. The tension in the pit stall went up a notch. It looked like Paolo's first "for real" pit stop was going to be under the green flag, which meant that it must be, had to be, perfect. Anything else would be disastrous.

Bear hopped off the war wagon and called the Ballet Company together. He wrapped his arms around the group, and they looked much like a football team in a huddle. He pushed the radio mouthpiece out of the way, looked them in the face, and spoke directly to them. "All right, you know what we gotta do. If we can get him out with that first group, he has a chance. You know we're gonna be spotting those other guys a second at least, so let's do this one quick and perfect. Ed, be sure you get all the fuel in. If this thing stays green, we'll need it. Paolo, be quick. We're counting on you." With that he turned back to the racetrack.

"OK, Orly, we are in the window. When the leaders pit, which they're going to do together, I want you to peel off and hit the pit lane. We're going to try to get you up there with them."

Orly's mike clicked twice.

Paolo stood just behind the pit wall with the jack in his hands. His mouth was dry. He put his worry aside—he was fast and he could do this.

Doug turned to Alicia on top of the transporter. They both had heard Bear's one-sided conversation with Orly. "Won't be long now," Doug said to her. She nodded and said a quiet prayer for Pally.

The waiting game was going on a little longer than most anticipated. Nobody wanted to pit first. Bear was getting worried. Lap fifty-five rolled by, then on lap fifty-six the leader of the pack threw up his hand, signaling that he was coming in. The next fifteen cars behind him followed suit, and suddenly the relative calmness of the pit lane was shattered as the cars peeled off turn four and slowed dramatically at the entrance to the pits. There was a mandated speed limit of 55 miles per hour in the pit lane. Exceed that and a driver faced a thirty-second penalty from NASCAR, which could drop him right out of contention in one hot minute. But after running nearly 200 miles per hour for all those laps, 55 miles per hour seemed like crawling, especially to guys who were in the midst of white-knuckle competition, jockeying to get in their pit stalls.

Jimmy and Bear spoke at the same time. "They're coming in, Orly. Come with them." Orly was still a couple of seconds back, and it gave him time to set the car up for the entrance to the pits. He came off the corner, entered the pit lane approach, and slowed to the mandated speed.

The three-foot orange and purple #37 pit sign hung over the pit stall on a long pole marking the edge of the stall. Orly brought the car in and slid it to stop dead on the mark, with the pit sign just touching the front of the car. The crewman immediately lifted the pole, and the Thunderfoot Ballet Company was over the wall in a blur of motion trailing air hoses behind them. Paolo laid the jack down perfectly and slid it under the car. One large pump and the car fairly leaped into the air. Bud and Bobby fired their air guns and lug nuts went flying. The old rubber was laid down on the ground, and the tire handlers helped place the new rubber on as the guns screamed in high-pitched agony once again as the lugs were tightened. Bud said, "Now," and Paolo dropped the car. He stepped out with his right foot in the classic pulling guard mode and made the cut around the front of the car to the right side. He slid the jack under the car once again and up it went. The air guns fired, the rubber came off and went back on. In the meantime, Ed emptied the first eleven-gallon gas can, pivoted on one leg, and threw it over the wall into waiting hands. The can no sooner left his hands than the second can was in his arms and slammed over the nozzle in the side of the car. Tim Markham, the catch man, had his little can over the vent spout for the gas tank. At first just air came rushing out, then a fine vapor of fuel, and finally a gush of gas, signaling that the tank was full. Paolo watched carefully and then Bud's voice barked in his ear again, "Now," and he dropped the jack, sliding it out of the way as Orly burned rubber, leaving the pit stall. It was a fast stop—a very fast stop—and every motion was captured by the network camera crew covering the event for the national audience.

The crew came back over the wall high-fiving and congratulating each other. Bear's voice came across their headsets. "Great job, guys—15.6 seconds. That was one fast stop. Everybody did great."

The roving pit reporter stuck his mike in Bear's face and asked him what he thought. Bear made the appropriate response and got back to work.

Orly eased down the pit lane at the mandated speed and then blasted through the gears onto the track. He built up momentum with the five or six cars behind him and a couple in front of him. It would take a couple of laps to get things sorted out, but maybe he picked up a few spots. It seemed like one heck of a stop. He focused on building speed and looked for yet another dancing partner.

Three laps later, he was sixteenth and in the middle of the 200-mile-per-hour freight train that made up the lead pack.

Doug looked over at Alicia, lifted his mouthpiece, and spoke to her directly. "That was one of the fastest pit stops ever for the Ballet Company. I told Paolo he could do it. He was flawless."

Alicia smiled and nodded her head. She knew he could do it too.

Juan-Jesus tugged her hand. "Alicia, they're talking about Orly Mann on the radio. They said that it was one of the fastest green-flag pit stops ever recorded. Can you tell me what this means?"

Alicia did her best to yell in his ear and finally ended up by saying that it was because Paolo was making the jack work and he was the best.

Juan-Jesus rolled his eyes and raised his arms, "Well, we all know that," he said. Then he said in English, "Ain't no big thang."

In the meantime, Bear was talking to himself. "Oh, we're in it now. Yes, thank you, Lord, we're in it now. Now we got a chance . . ." He walked back and forth wiping his hands on the red shop rag in his back pocket. "Race ain't even half over and we're in it now."

Orly settled in and bided his time. The car was still working good. The push had disappeared, for the moment at least, with the fresh tires. He knew that as the fuel load lightened and the tires wore, it would be back. In the meantime, he settled in and did his best to stay in the draft. He eased his body into his seat and tried to relax. He took a couple of swallows from the tube to his water bottle and checked his gauges. He was in good shape for now and so was the car.

On the next lap disaster struck. Orly dropped off the banking on turn four and felt the engine flutter, then hesitate just a fraction. His foot was buried on the floor, but the car was slowing. He glanced at the tach. Sure enough, the revs were dropping. He went high through the tri-oval as the freight train left him in the dust.

Bear's voice barked in his ear. "Talk to me, Orly."

"Don't know yet, Bear, but I'm losing revs," Orly said as he lost another six or seven spots. He was staying high, up out of the groove. If the motor seized up, he didn't want to be in the middle of the pack. He would most likely dump a load of oil and coolant on the track, and it not only could but likely would set off a chain reaction that could take out half the field. Things had been remarkably calm on the track so far. No need to upset the apple cart.

Bear's mind was working frantically. "Orly, when you get a chance switch the box and see if that helps."

Orly clicked the mike twice. Bear was talking about the electronic box that controlled the spark to the ignition. It sent out over thirty thousand volts, and because it was such a delicate mechanism, a backup system was built right alongside it. If the voltage dropped for some reason, the engine would not be able to put out the power it was capable of. All Orly needed was the opportunity to look down and flip the proper switches. Considering the speed and the proximity to the other race cars around him, Orly needed to time his actions carefully. He got the car pointed down the back chute and watched in dismay as the cars ahead of him simply outran him. No amount of draft would work if you didn't have the power to stay hooked up. He glanced down and flipped the switches. It was almost like he cut in the afterburner on a fighter jet. The power came right back, and he watched the tach out of the corner of his eye as he built up more speed.

"Yeah, that was it, Bear. Musta been something in the box. The revs came right back up, and it's running better than it was before." Orly went on. "What'd that cost us, Doug?"

"Well, you're back in twenty-fourth, and the lead draft is pulling away from you . . ."

Doug was interrupted by Jimmy's voice, "Yellow flag, Orly, yellow flag . . . somebody behind you lost an engine and oiled down the track. Race 'em back to the flag."

Once a driver crossed the start-finish line and the waving yellow flag, he could not improve his position but up to the line anything was possible. Orly picked up a couple of spots just as he crossed the line and lifted his foot.

"The oil's in turn two. They should have it cleaned up fairly quick," said Jimmy.

Bear motioned to the crew to get ready. "Orly, as soon as they open the pits, follow the leaders in. We're on lap ninety-five. We're in the window for fuel and tires."

Orly's mike clicked twice.

"What else you need?"

Orly's mike clicked twice, which meant nothing—don't touch a thing.

Once again the orange and yellow machine came thundering down the pit lane. Even though it was a yellow-flag stop, it still had to be perfect. If they could get Orly out quick, he would be back up in the lead pack again.

The Ballet Company went over the wall in fluidlike motion that belied their speed. Paolo threw the jack under the car and it went up like magic.

Bud was on his knees knocking lug nuts off when two cars tangled trying to get into their stalls. The pit lane was wide, but it wasn't wide enough for three cars to run side by side. One driver was a little hot coming in and locked his brakes. When he did, he hit a very small patch of moisture from someone's overheated radiator, and the hot, slick racing tires lost traction. The car spun 180 degrees sideways with the nose pointing right into Orly's pit stall. As the car slid by, it clipped the tire that Bud had just laid down. The tire bounced into Bud and pinned him against Orly's fender. Paolo was just about to drop the jack when he sensed more than felt the car slide by him, missing his feet and the jack handle by inches. The driver refired his car and backed up a foot, which freed the tire and unpinned Bud. Paolo was about to let go of the jack and run to help when he remembered Tyrone's words. Carl Henry, the front-tire handler, was right there anyway. Paolo waited. Before he could drop the jack, the lug nuts had to be tight. For every pit stall there was a NASCAR official, and one of his main jobs was to see that all the lug nuts were on tight before a car left the pits. The NASCAR official was standing there watching. Bear's voice blasted in Paolo's ear. "Are they tight, Bud?" Bud gave a wave of his hand and got to his feet. Paolo dropped the jack and sprinted to the left side of the car. Bud followed behind him. The whole incident only took a second or two, but it was enough to slow the Ballet Company a little. They got Orly out in decent time, but he was still back in the pack.

As they went back over the wall, Bud put his arms around Paolo's shoulders. "Thanks for watching, Paolo. If you woulda dropped the jack, the tire would have crushed my arm. When he hit the tire it wedged me under the fender. Sharp thinking. Thanks."

The other members of the crew slapped him on the back. Paolo just nodded. It was too much to think about right now. Later, when this thing was over, he would reflect on the strange sensation of a sliding, 3600-pound stock car brushing across the seat of his pants. Man, that was close! At least Bud was OK.

Bear's voice echoed in the headsets. "Everybody OK? Good. You guys did great. Man, that idiot almost made me have to go hire a whole new pit crew." Everybody laughed.

Doug breathed a sigh of relief. From his vantage point he couldn't see the right side of the car, but when the other car broke loose and went sliding by Orly's car sideways he knew how close it must have been to his dad and Paolo.

The yellow flag only lasted four laps and then it was green-green-green, go-go-go again. Orly settled in and tried to make up ground. At least for the moment he could see the leaders up there somewhere. But then maybe he couldn't. The whole pack was tightened up right now, and restarts were the most dangerous part of restrictor-plate racing. Everybody was so bunched together there was no room for error. If one guy made a mistake, he was going to take some others with him. That was a given.

Jimmy was watching critically from his perch high above the track. His experienced eye told him that the boys were getting tired of playing nice. The lead had see-sawed back and forth among eight different cars, and as the laps wound down it was getting time to play some serious hardball. The draft was tightening up and there was some serious bumping going on. At 200 miles per hour, even a light touch was enough to loosen somebody in a corner. Something was going to give pretty soon. He could smell it coming. Orly was stuck right in the middle of the field. If somebody spun, there would be some serious shucking and jiving going on.

"Watch yourself, Orly. They're starting to rub door handles up front." It was a slang expression because the slick body styles had no door handles, or even doors for that matter.

Orly's mike clicked twice. He could feel it too. The intensity on the track was building. This race was still up for grabs. No one had seriously dominated anyone else, and right now the million bucks, plus some change, for first place was up for grabs. A lot of championship points were at stake as well. Orly had to decide whether now was the time to be superaggressive or the time to back off a little and play it safe.

It was a question he didn't have to ponder for long because it was answered for him. The answer came suddenly, but when it came it seemed to last forever. The cars currently running fourth and fifth touched in the middle of turns one and two. They drifted apart in the air current and then slammed into each other like they had been sucked together. The impact caused them both to pirouette in lazy circles, collecting other cars as they spun up the track. Then both of them slammed into the wall, ricocheting back across the track toward the infield grass, trailing bent and twisted sheet metal with them. It takes a long time to scrub off a speed of 195 miles per hour. These two cars were at the front, which meant that they had thirty-odd cars behind them bunched up, running nose to tail.

Orly's world went gray with tire smoke, and Jimmy became his guardian angel and flight controller at the same time. "Stay low, stay low, stay low." Orly stayed low and flashed by the spinning cars only to be plunged into more weirdness as other cars ran into each other and spun in their own fluids. Jimmy's voice spoke again, "Move up, move up, move up . . . hang in there . . . you got it . . . watch the oil . . . watch the oil . . . there's some loose debris below you . . . stay in the center groove . . . watch it!"

Orly flinched as a car came off the wall directly in front of him backward with its roof flaps up. He resisted the impulse to slow down. If he checked up, somebody would tag him in the rear for sure. There was a sharp "tink" as he flashed past. Orly's car jumped sideways in the oil as he lost traction, but he held it down and chased it up the track toward the wall with quick flicks of the steering wheel and easing out of the gas. He got the car back under him just as he was about out of room and put his foot back into the throttle.

Jimmy broke in again. "You're OK, Orly. I think you got through clean. Get to the yellow flag. I think we can pick up some spots here in a hurry."

Orly pointed the car down the back straight using every bit of his experience to make sure all the pieces were where they belonged. He hoped he hadn't run over any debris. He didn't want to cut a tire at 200 miles per hour. Even with the inner liner it could mean a wild ride. He flashed across the start-finish line to take the yellow flag and gently eased off the gas as a good portion of the field came up behind him.

Juan-Jesus happened to be watching the leaders when the crash started. He let out a yell and pointed as the race-track erupted in tire smoke and spinning cars. Both Doug and Alicia watched with open mouths as they heard Jimmy's voice calmly directing Orly through the melee.

Bear never watched too much more than his own car and the pit lane during the course of a race, so he had his back to the wreck. He was watching Orly in the middle of the pack when things came apart. He'd been wondering what they were going to do to get Orly up in the lead group, and now old Mr. Opportunity had just come a knockin'.

He made sure that Orly was through the mess and then he turned to the Ballet Company once again. "OK, here's the break we been looking for. Let's make this next stop quick, but be real careful to look him over good. If you see anything, let me know as quick as you can. Bud? You OK? You want me to fill in for you?"

Bud laughed. "No, Bear, I don't. I'm OK." There was a chorus of assent from the rest of the crew.

Orly came down the pit lane once again. This time the stop was quick and without incident. Bud ran a gloved hand over the grille opening in the front of the car, knocking away any debris that might keep air flowing to the radiator. Everybody had a good look around the car and reported no damage, except for a slight crease on the left-rear quarter panel. That must have been the "tink" Orly had heard.

Orly accelerated out of the pits with fresh tires and a full load of fuel. He lined up behind the pace car on the outside in seventh place.

The pit lane looked like a triage ward on the edge of a battlefield as the crews tried to straighten and fix what they could to get the damaged cars back on the track. Daytona might be the Great American Race and all that, but it was still the first race of the season and points were points. There were thirty-three races left on the schedule, and any kind of finish here might pay off later. It never ceased to amaze Alicia that these cars, which were so lovingly massaged to make them slip through the air, were now having their bodies adjusted by hammers and pry bars and held together with racers' tape.

"How many laps left, Doug?" asked Orly

As always Doug was ready. "Sixty-one, Orly. You're currently in seventh. The lapped cars will start beside you, and there are twenty-one . . . no, there are twenty cars on the lead lap. On that last run your times were consistent with the leaders and so far, nobody has been able to stay out front for very long."

Orly's mike clicked twice as the starter gave the "One to go" signal, which meant the green flag would come out the next time around.

"Bear, we got enough fuel?" asked Orly.

"Don't know yet, Orly," which meant that Bear was in the process of finding out. He was busy calibrating fuel mileage with Ed. Ed and the catch man, Tim, kept track of exactly how much fuel they had put in the car by weighing the cans after every stop. They would give Bear a good estimate on the mileage he was getting. He hoped he had the carb jetted right.

Bear got back to Orly. "I'll let you know but don't worry about it. We're getting mileage that's as good as anybody, so if one stops then everybody will have to."

Orly's mike clicked twice.

The green flag came out, and the seven cars were locked together in single-file with Orly bringing up the rear. *Here's where the real dancing starts,* thought Orly. *It's every man for himself and none for all.* He snuggled up to the car in front of him and weaved a little to take some of the air off the guy's spoiler. It took a little downforce off him, and Orly watched him chase the car up the track. Orly ducked below him and settled into sixth. The other driver pulled down behind Orly, and Orly got ready for the same move. *Now is when the handling characteristics of this good car might really pay off.* He wasn't all that fast in a straight line, but the car was stable. He felt a light tap as the driver behind him pulled up and tried the same move. Orly's car wiggled a little but didn't get loose. Orly smiled. *Yup, now it was time to really go racin'.*

Jimmy spoke, "You all right?"

Orly's mike clicked twice.

Jimmy spoke again. "Watch yourself, Orly. The wind is starting to pick up coming off of two."

Do not withhold good from those who deserve it, when it is in your power to act.

Proverbs 3:27

"It's a little tense out there. When they gave that last restart, some of the guys who wanted you to draft with them would have been like playing catch with a hand grenade."

Kenny Schrader, Winston Cup driver, car #33

THE CROWD WAS on its feet. The seven cars had distanced themselves from the rest of the field but they were as close together as seven cars could be. Periodically someone would think about pulling out and going for the lead, but if no one pulled out with him they would lose the draft and fall behind. Once a driver lost the lead draft, there would be no way to catch up unless the second group of cars caught up to help. By that time the lead group would be long gone. It had turned into a 200-mile-per-hour chess game, and every driver thought he had the winning move.

Orly was no exception. His car was starting to show wear. The push was back and this time it was a little stronger. He compensated by using a lower line, but it was only a matter of time until it got worse. The temp was starting to go up a little as well. Every so often he would have to ease out from behind the car in front of him and let some fresh air run through the grille. When a driver drafted another car for any length of time, he wasn't getting the circulation around the radiator he needed to cool the engine.

"How many, Doug?"

"Thirty-one, Orly." The lap countdown continued. Orly bided his time and then Jimmy's voice spoke in his ear.

"Yellow flag, Orly! Yellow flag! Somebody just hit the wall coming off four. He's high up against the wall. Watch yourself."

Orly threw his hand in the air to let the driver behind know that he might be slowing. The wrecked car was up against the wall with a trickle of fluid leaking from underneath it. Everybody stayed in line and behaved himself. *It is still too soon to be heroic,* thought Orly. The pack flashed under the starter's box glued together. Orly eased up on the gas.

"Talk to me, Bear," said Orly.

"Do what the rest of 'em do, Orly. You want four or two?" Bear was talking about tires.

"It doesn't matter if they come in or not. I have to and you better give me four. My push is back and it's getting tighter. Give me a little air pressure adjustment. You know what to do. Tell the guys they've done a great job today, but this one has got to be right."

Bear did indeed know what to do and in fact had already done it. The next set of tires would reflect the change. It would help but not alleviate the problem. But Bear and Orly's conversation did exactly what Bear and Orly hoped it would do. They knew the other guys were listening, just like Doug was listening to them. When Orly made the decision to pit, it made the choice easy for them. The truth was that nobody had enough fuel to go the distance, and now the race would not only be run on the track, it would be run in the pits as well. The first car out would be in the lead, and if the stop was mishandled the driver might find himself back in the pack and out of the big money.

The pit lane was open for business, and Orly brought the car down at precisely 55 miles per hour, no more, but certainly no less. He slid to a stop and this time the Ballet Company outdid themselves. Paolo was poetry in motion and the air hoses snaked out behind Bud and Bobby. They were over the wall like orange and purple cats and hit the ground sliding on their knee pads, the air guns screaming before they stopped sliding. There was no wasted motion, no superfluous energy, just quick and sudden movement. Then boom, the jack was down and Orly hit the pavement with the car in gear and the tires spinning. He snaked out of the pit stall, leaving big black streaks of rubber on the pavement and tire smoke hanging in the air. There were two cars right with him, and it was neck and neck as they exited the pit lane. Orly ducked into second behind the pace car. He keyed the mike.

"Great stop, guys, great stop. That was awesome."

This time there was no high-fiving in the pits. Things were just too intense. No one was talking. Even Bear was standing still for once.

For four more laps they followed the pace car. The front seven was now reduced to six. One car was still back in the pits with a broken transmission and a driver pounding the steering wheel in frustration. The rest of the pack had pulled up behind this lead group under the yellow, but virtually everyone knew that these were the guys to beat. Orly was in second and he was happy.

"How many, Doug?"

"Seventeen laps, Orly. It's just the front group now. The rest of the field is just hanging in there, I think. You front guys are the fastest, so when the green drops . . ."

Orly's mike clicked twice. He took a few deep breaths and calmed himself. This was the part he loved. Some guys got nervous at this point. It was the most pressure a guy could imagine. Sixteen laps left, and there was nobody between him and the checkered flag except the guy in front of him. It was time to go to war, which is precisely how the other five drivers were feeling. The battle had been long and furious. They had been slugging it out for nearly three hours and now it was the final act. Orly was wet with sweat, and the once pristine race car was showing the stress of combat. There was a black donut on the left side of the car from some inadvertent contact with the tire of another racer. The paint on the front end of the car was chipped and blistered from constant contact with tiny pebbles and sand pulled up from the racing surface. The grille was slightly pushed in from the contact Orly had made when he bump drafted into the lead. Orly's windshield was also pocked and streaked with oil and coolant. But the car still had some left and Orly meant to get every ounce of it.

The front group tightened up until they were literally touching each other as the pace car brought them around once more. The leader was just a few feet behind the pace car and creeping up as they gained speed. The cameraman shooting footage from the backseat of the pace car was swallowing hard to keep his concentration. He hoped that the retired stock car driver steering this thing knew his business. These guys were serious, and they better be out of the way when the green flag fell or they would flat get run over. My, oh my, but they were close!

The six cars were nose to tail with no room between them as the starter nervously held the green flag behind his leg, out of sight. The driver did know his business, and the pace car once again dived for the safety of the pits. All six drivers slapped the floorboards at the same time. The crowd was on its feet, and they roared as the cars flashed beneath the starter wildly waving the green flag.

Orly stayed tucked in behind the leader, literally pushing him as they came out of turn two. The third and fourth cars hooked up together and ducked low to the inside to see if they could make the pass around Orly and the leader. They pulled even but that was it. They couldn't pull it off. The pack built speed as they picked up momentum. Orly sailed into the thirty-one-degree banking, looking down into the fourth place car who was right beside him. He could have stuck his hand out the window and touched the other car. It was now up to the fifth- and sixth-place cars behind them. If they tucked in behind the inside two, Orly and the leader would quickly be relegated to the end of the group; but if they tucked in behind Orly and the leader, then they would be able to pull ahead. They did neither. One tucked in behind the inside group and the other tucked in behind Orly.

From the fans' perspective it looked as if the cars were running in tight formation. Inside the cars it was much different. The afternoon breeze was playing havoc with the airflow from the drafting cars. It was pushing them all over the place, and each car was bobbing and weaving in unexpected two-foot increments. Occasionally, they would touch coming off a corner and lightly tap each other in the rear. The drivers were doing their best, but keeping the cars precise was impossible. It was not a game for the fainthearted. All six drivers had their feet nailed to the floorboards. Any little mistake, any lack of concentration, any miscalculation, any sudden lapse of courage . . . could be disastrous.

They ran this way for nearly ten laps, and not one of the thousands of spectators at the speedway could sit down. No one had ever—in the history of NASCAR—seen such tight racing for such a long period of time. Six of the most talented drivers in the world were doing everything in their power to get by each other, but nothing was working.

Then, as was bound to happen, somebody bobbled a little coming off the corner. Perhaps it was a loss of nerve or an errant gust of wind, but whatever it was it shuffled the group and gave Orly a chance to get to the inside, which is where he desperately wanted to be. Now he could run the low groove, and it was here his car was working best. The push was coming back, but now maybe he could use it to his advantage. He took a quick look in his mirror to see which driver was behind him.

"He'll come, Orly. Go for it," said Jimmy. He knew exactly what Orly was planning and so did Bear. Bear was no longer walking back and forth. He was standing on top of the war wagon, making himself dizzy as he spun in a circle trying to follow the cars around the two-and-a-half-mile tri-oval in tiny steps. Paolo and the rest of the crew alternated from watching the six-car train go by on the front stretch and then running to the TV monitor to see the rest of the lap. The Thunderfoot Ballet Company was done for now. They were spectators, like the thousands of others who were glued to the action. It was purely up to Orly.

Doug's voice echoed in everybody's headset, "Ten left, Orly, ten."

He would give Orly the count. The starter was also holding up ten fingers as they flashed by.

Orly flew down the back chute, then made his move. He slipped up to the lead car and bumped him slightly, then weaved just enough to get under him and take a little air off his spoiler as they entered turn three. Then he ducked low, as much as he dared, to put his left-front tire almost on the apron, the flat area just below the banking. A car could make the corner going flat out if it was on the banking, but if it touched the flat part of the racetrack it would upset the balance of the car, making it spin. That was a given. It was like a roller-blader running off the sidewalk into the grass. Orly had maybe six inches and no more to spare. The lead driver knew the drill as well as Orly, and he tried to cheat down on him by crowding him onto the apron.

What no one counted on was the fact that there was a car just exiting the pit lane. He was one of the unfortunate ones caught up in the "Wreck," and his once beautiful car was now a rolling piece of junk. He had been in and out of the pits and was just trying to run enough laps to collect some valuable points. He was low on the apron and doing his best to gain enough speed to pull up onto the racing surface. He was having trouble getting up to speed, which meant that Orly and the rest were closing in on him at over 100 miles per hour. Orly had to make a split-second decision: keep his foot in it and run the risk of making a tremendous mess right there in the tri-oval by smacking into the back of the wounded car or back off and slip back up behind the leader. If he backed off, there was every likelihood the car lurking three inches behind him would plow into him, spinning everybody. He couldn't back off. Orly tightened his jaw and kept his foot flat to the floor while two things happened. The first was that the wounded duck coming out of the pits swerved to the left, off the banking and practically into the grass when his spotter yelled in his ear and he saw the pack flying up behind him. The second was that the leader, still trying to regroup after being touched by Orly, inadvertently moved up the track, giving him just barely the room he needed.

Orly took the lead!

Now if he could just hold it.

"Nine laps, Orly. Nice move."

Nice move indeed, thought Bear as he mopped his sweating forehead. "Oh, I like racin'. Yes, indeed, I truly do, but why, oh why, do you have to scare me like that, Orly Mann?" said Bear to no one in particular. He realized he was holding his breath and forced himself to breathe.

The other drivers tried. First it was the car that helped Orly take the lead by sticking so close to him. He tried the same trick on Orly and did everything he could to take the air off Orly's spoiler and move him up the track. But Orly's car was more stable and it wasn't easy to move him. Orly played the blocking game, making the car as wide as possible.

Then the boys in back got into the game and tried to get by him one by one. They fell back a little and made a run at him off the corner, but again Orly was able to hold them off. Jimmy kept his mouth shut and only spoke when he thought he could help. Orly needed every ounce of concentration he could muster. He was what athletes often call "in the zone," and he was so deep into driving that the world could end and he would never know it. His whole focus was the car and the ribbon of asphalt that unwound before him. Every bump and wind current impacted his consciousness as he squeezed the steering wheel to keep the car exactly where he wanted it. The cars behind him were the enemy and he couldn't let them get by.

Orly was actually surprised when the starter waved the white flag, one lap to go. He hunkered down in the seat and refused to think. He just drove. The final assault came going into turn one, and he felt the solid tap on his rear bumper as the second-place car tried to loosen him up for a pass once again. Actually it was more than a tap, it

225

was a solid hit and it loosened Orly enough to allow the third-place car to get in the mix. As they flew down the back chute for the final time, they were running three wide. Orly held the low line as the looming turn three approached. They sailed into the corner together, and now all six cars were running three abreast. There was no way they were all going to get through the corner like this. Orly stayed low as the outside car crept by him and the car outside of him clipped the wall. He didn't hit it hard but it was enough. The car behind him tapped him lightly in his unbalanced state, and then everybody was sliding in great clouds of tire smoke.

Orly came off the corner sideways and did a pirouette off the corner into the dogleg. The car spun 360 degrees once and then spun again. This time around Orly caught it on the fly, banged third gear, and accelerated to take the checkered flag with the other competitors as the pack came thundering up behind them.

The racetrack erupted into pandemonium. It was the closest Daytona 500 ever. Bear, in his excitement, fell off the pit wall and missed the finish.

Orly slowed going into turn one and dropped his window net. He looked at the driver in the car next to him and mouthed the words, "Who won?" The driver looked back at him with a grin and raised both hands off the wheel in a gesture that said, "Don't know."

"Hang on, Orly," said Doug in his ear in a hoarse voice. "It was so close that NASCAR is reviewing the tape." There was a long pause as Orly idled down the back chute, collecting himself. Then Doug spoke again.

"Hey, Orly. We just won the Daytona 500."

The Thunderfoot Ballet Company was pounding each other on the back. Bear was limping in circles and receiving the congratulations from the other teams. Everybody was saying the same thing, "What a race, what a race, what a fantastic race!"

Orly came idling off the track and up the pit lane with his hand out the window, slapping palms as he headed toward winner's circle. The Thunderfoot Ballet Company swarmed around him and pounded on the car as he crept along. Then he pulled into victory circle and killed the engine.

Doug, Alicia, and Juan-Jesus came running up to join the celebration. It was a wild time. Orly was interviewed by twenty different media folks. He dutifully changed sponsor hats for the PR pictures and said all the appropriate words, thanking his sponsors and crew. Bear and Orly had their picture taken with a large facsimile of the winner's check. Then the Ballet Company had their picture taken, and Paolo couldn't keep the smile off his face. This racin' stuff was fun, especially when you won!

After an hour the crowd began to thin. Paolo was standing next to Alicia, Juan-Jesus, and Doug when Orly and Bear walked up. Juan-Jesus was solemn as he studied Orly from a distance. Then he edged a little closer and extended his right hand to Orly.

Orly reached down, took Juan-Jesus's hand, shook it gently, and said, "*Con mucho gusto, mi amigo.* I've heard a great deal about you."

Juan-Jesus replied, "*Con mucho gusto, Señor Orly.* You're one *mas grande hombre.*"

"And so are you, my friend, and so are you."

The twin-engine aircraft dropped smoothly to the tarmac late Monday evening at the dusty little airport in Calexico. It was on the outskirts of town and so close to the border that you could throw a rock into Mexico. The plane taxied to the end of the runway, turned around, and pulled over to the small passenger terminal. An older man and a younger woman were standing together, waiting with a couple of small suitcases at their feet. With them were two young girls, one of them jumping up and down in excitement. The younger of the two girls was sitting in a wheelchair and looked very tired, but she still had a smile on her face. As the turboprop motors shut down, the side door of the airplane flew open, and Juan-Jesus hit the ground running. He flew across the pavement into the arms of the waiting woman. Alicia and Orly Mann followed.

Juan-Jesus hugged his mother and kissed her cheek. Then he hugged both of his sisters as all four of them wept together.

Alicia walked up and shook hands with the older man. "Pastor Rojas, it is so good to see you again. This is my friend, Mr. Orly Mann." Orly shook his hand and smiled. Then Juan-Jesus took Orly's hand and introduced him to his mother and sisters. His mom was very shy in the presence of such a great man, but she looked him in the face and said, *"Gracias, Señor Mann,"* with heartfelt emotion. She gave Alicia a hug, and they patted each other in a gesture of women who respect each other.

They talked with Pastor Rojas for a few minutes, then bid him *adios* as Orly and Alicia ushered Juan-Jesus's mother and sisters onto the airplane. Juan-Jesus was jabbering like a monkey and reassuring his family that flying was perfectly OK. Orly Mann was not only the best race car driver in the world, he was also the best pilot, and the flight to San Diego wouldn't take long at all.

A few minutes later, the airplane taxied to the end of the runway and took off into the evening darkness.

EPILOGUE

Run in such a way as to get the prize.

1 Corinthians 9:24b

ON TUESDAY EVENING Paolo called Alicia at her home in San Francisco. She was waiting for his call.

"Are you guys still on cloud nine?" she asked.

"No . . . well, maybe a little. The truth is that we're working our tails off getting ready for Rockingham. That's the amazing thing about this sport. You just get done and then you start all over again," said Paolo. "So, tell me, how did it all go?"

"They're waiting for results. Orly flew us to San Diego and they picked everybody up at the airport. He made the arrangements, I guess. Then this morning they went to the hospital for tests and all that stuff. It looks like Juan-Jesus is going to be a match, but it's too soon to tell if it will help Angelica. We need to pray very hard," said Alicia. "Then we flew to San Francisco after we dropped them off, and here I am. . . . But, Pally, I have some interesting news."

"What? Tell me."

"When I got home, my folks took me aside and told me that they're moving to Florida . . . to Orlando, actually. My dad has been promoted and so they're moving."

"What about your Aunty Grandmother, the one living in San Francisco? Man, she's going to be lost without you guys."

"She's moving too. In fact, she's already sold the restaurant and she's moving in with my other Aunty Grandmothers. It seems that this whole thing has been in the works for quite some time, and no one bothered to tell me." Alicia said this last part with a sharp tone in her voice.

"They probably didn't want to worry you, Alicia. Maybe they were concerned about how you might respond. Speaking of that, how do you feel about the whole thing?"

"I'm not sure, Pally, but now I have another complication. Orly has offered me a job in Charlotte. He wants me to come in and set up the computer system and work with Helen at the office at his shop."

"You mean here? Here in Charlotte? Wow, Alicia, what are you going to do? Man, that's neat."

"I don't know yet, Pally. I could stay here in the city with friends and still go to school. But all my family's going to be in Florida. I still have to think about it and pray about it. I just found out. I'm flying back to Florida with Orly and some business people on Thursday, and then in a week I'll fly back here with Aunty Grandmother. I don't know, Pally. I'm a little mixed up right now."

"Yeah, I understand, Alicia. I sorta know how you feel. I'll be praying for you."

They talked for a long time—there was a lot to talk about—but finally it was time to go. Alicia bid Paolo good-bye and hung up the phone. *Charlotte. I wonder what it would be like to live in Charlotte? I'll see the folks occasionally when we travel to Florida to race,* she thought. *Decision? Ha, what decision? Thank you, Lord.*

Orly came into the shop on Friday morning. He was tired but feeling good. What a week! He walked into Bear's office and sat down. Bear was sitting behind the computer console checking some numbers. Behind him was a large glass window that looked out into the ultramodern, super-clean shop. There was a lot of activity going on, but the soundproof glass kept the noise out.

"Well, Mr. Daytona 500 winner, howzit going?"

"Going good, Bear. Landed late last night. Got the Mendoza family all set up. Don't know if the match will work yet, but they got the best working on it."

"Did you get the fund set up OK?"

"Yeah, I worked through some lawyers at our sponsor's home office. I did like we decided. I put two hundred thousand of the winnings into the fund. Mrs. Mendoza can draw what she needs. She hasn't made up her mind whether she'll move to the States permanently yet, but she has to stay for a while so Angelica can get her treatments. This hospital is the best in dealing with this stuff. She's going to put Juan-Jesus in a Christian school close to where they're living, and they'll teach him English and help him make the transition. He told me through Alicia that he doesn't need to go to school, that he'll learn to be a locksmith like his papa. We talked a long time and I think we convinced him to go to school. What a kid!"

"Yeah, he's a pretty sharp cookie, all right. Is Alicia going to come and help me straighten out this mess of a computer? Doug says she's a crackerjack."

"She's still thinking about it but I think she will."

"Well, there's one big curly headed young man out there who's a hopin' and prayin'," Bear chuckled.

"Hey, how's Tyrone doing?" Orly asked.

"Well, so far so good. He's workin' hard and keepin' his mouth shut. We'll see how it works out. He and Paolo and Doug have become pretty good friends. Don't know if that's good or bad, but I think it's mostly good."

"Now we got to figure out a way to get John and Martha to give up that raggedy old motor home and get them in something a little newer," said Orly.

"You know, that won't be easy," said Bear.

"Hey, Bear?"

"Yeah, Orly?"

"What a race. Man, that was something to see and I was in it."

"Yes, indeedy, you were in it. Oh, I love racin', yes, I do."

Stay tuned for the next Thunderfoot Ballet Company Adventures with the Orly Mann Racing Team.